CRUEL VICTIM

by the same
author

A Charmed Death

CRUEL VICTIM

Miles Tripp

St. Martin's Press
New York

Library of Congress Cataloging in Publication Data

Tripp, Miles, 1923–
    Cruel victim.

    I. Title.
PR6070.R48C7   1985   823'.914   85-2561
ISBN 0-312-17769-0

First published in Great Britain by Macmillan London Ltd.

First U.S. Edition

10 9 8 7 6 5 4 3 2 1

AUTHOR'S NOTE

Although it is well known that some religious sects use manipulative techniques which amount to brainwashing to establish dominance over new members, who are usually young people, it is not perhaps quite so well known that some parents in the USA have employed self-styled 'deprogramming technicians' to reverse the effects of religious brainwashing.

Whilst the characters in this book are fictitious, the information about methods used by technicians, from the time their 'subject' is kidnapped until he or she has been reconverted, is factual. It is to be hoped that deprogramming does not become acceptable in Europe. There are already too many forms of mind-manipulation in current use throughout the world without adding to the list.

M.T.

CHAPTER ONE

With short legs and massive body, and a skin resembling hide, Samson was used to unflattering remarks about his appearance. And if someone had told him, as he sat listening to the play-back of a tape-recorder, that he looked more like a sleepy hippopotamus than an alert private detective in search of a clue, he would probably have agreed. He found his latest case rather boring. An author, convinced that his notes for a history of silhouette artists had been stolen and sold to a competitor, had instructed Samson to find evidence to support this belief.

After a while Samson switched off the tape-recorder. He wished profoundly that the camera had been invented a century earlier. Etienne de Silhouette would then have been out of business before he started, and the world, and Samson, would have been spared tedious histories of artists who made a living from drawing black profiles on white paper.

He pressed a button on his desk and his secretary came in.

'Have we got anything else today, Shandy?'

'A Mr Camber is coming to see you at three.'

'What does he want?'

'Missing person.'

Samson gave a prodigious yawn. 'Another household object that has somehow got mislaid?'

'This one might be different.'

'Why?'

'Having worked with you for three years I know how fed up you get with missing-person cases and so I made a few enquiries of my own before fixing the appointment.'

He smiled and revealed tiny, brilliantly white teeth set in gums of a pink which was so definitive it could have been used by stamp cataloguers and the house of Schiaparelli. 'I don't know what I'd do without you,' he said blandly.

'I'm afraid you'll have to learn to do without me. I've got some news to break to you.'

'What?'

'First things first. I'll tell you why this case might be different. It isn't about someone who has voluntarily gone missing. A girl has been abducted.'

'That's a police matter.'

'There are reasons for not bringing in the police. It isn't an abduction for sexual or political motives, apparently. Nor is it a kidnapping for a ransom. That's all I know.'

Samson stroked the second of his double chins. 'It might be interesting,' he said. 'Now then. What's this news you've got?'

Before marriage her name had been Elaine Shandy and 'Shandy' was what he called her although her married name was Bullivant. In the same way she always used his surname when she spoke to him and only prefixed it with a 'Mister' when a client was present. She had long fair hair which sometimes fell over her eyes and had to be scooped back. Her nose was a shade too big, and her lips a shade

8

too thin, to make her beautiful by present-day standards but in the days of Garbo she would have attracted envy and photographers.

She took a deep breath. 'This is going to be a shock. I'm expecting a baby.'

'I forbid it.'

'I am.'

'It's a dreadful mistake. Change your doctor. He's a fool.'

'Sorry, Samson.'

He made a pretence of looking closely at a calendar. 'We're in October, aren't we? It isn't the first of April?'

'No joke.'

'But you're original. Someone different from the herd. Why do you have to have a baby? Why can't you have something useful like a clock?'

She gave him a tender smile. 'My dear, if you had been the father I'm sure we'd have produced a darling little clock.'

He smiled back. There was so much he liked about her that the thought of losing her was like losing an arm. She was determined without being strident, intelligent without intellectual pride, and she could assess his moods and anticipate his wishes. Although she was twenty years his junior she could play a mothering role when he was depressed, and she knew how to amuse him. And all this had been achieved without a single sexual signal being transmitted by either.

'Is there anything else?' she asked.

'No, thanks.' He glanced at the watches strapped to his wrist. 'Our new client will be here soon. You'd better get back.'

*

'Mr Camber,' she said, ushering in a small, stout man with a well-trimmed white moustache and slightly bulbous grey eyes.

'Have a seat, Mr Camber,' said Samson, reaching for a notepad and pencil. Although the invitation to take a seat seemed nothing more than a polite formality he reckoned to learn something about a client from the chair selected and the manner of sitting. Camber took the middle of three upright chairs and brought it up to the desk so that he could sit facing Samson and with a minimum of space between them. Having done this, he glanced round the room, observing a number of clocks and bookcases. He then gave Samson a sharp look of doubt before composing his features into the sort of implacable blankness which characterises professional card-players and others who are determined not to reveal the whole truth.

'One or two questions before we get down to the problem,' said Samson. 'Your full name and address?'

'Richard Edward Camber. Your secretary has my address.'

'Major Camber?'

'Colonel, actually. Retired. How did you guess?'

'A shot in the dark.'

'My bearing and manner, I suppose. Can't shake off thirty years of training and discipline.'

'That must be it. I wouldn't have been surprised if you'd told me this room was in a shambles and I'd better get cracking on a tidying-up operation. Tell me, were you recommended by someone or did you see my advertisement in one of the legal periodicals?'

'Chap called Freeman mentioned you. Medical journalist. Expert on fringe medicines and whatnot. Knows a bit about brainwashing too. Made me very worried about

something. The fate of my grand-daughter to be precise.'
He stared straight at Samson. 'I'd like to take this point by
point.'

'Please do.'

'First, I must make it clear that I've sounded out the
police and, to put it bluntly, they don't give a damn. They
regard it as some sort of domestic issue and don't want
to touch it.'

Samson nodded understandingly. It was because the
police were shy of certain sorts of domestic dispute that
he was unlikely to go out of business.

'That is point one. Point two is that my daughter and
son-in-law don't know I've come to see you. Hell to pay
if they did. Be shot at dawn. It's their daughter, my grand-
daughter, who is missing. At least, they may know where
she is, but I certainly don't, and I want to. That's why I'm
here. Are you clear so far?'

'I've understood every word perfectly without having
the faintest idea what you're leading to.'

'Good man,' said the colonel. 'Point three. Family background. I don't like doing this, you understand. Goes right
against the grain discussing family matters with a stranger,
but Caroline's welfare is at stake.' He reached into a
pocket and after putting on gold-rimmed spectacles he
produced a photograph which he studied sadly before
handing it to Samson. 'That's her. Caroline Moore. Age
nineteen.'

The picture showed the head and shoulders of a pretty
girl whose most striking feature was long auburn hair.

'May I keep this?'

'Certainly. Brought it for you.' Camber removed his
spectacles and continued. 'Her father is a company director.
Big firm. Exports heavy-duty vehicles to all parts of the

world. Self-made chap who's done damn well but – hate having to say this – he and Caro have always fought like cat and dog. Mabel, my daughter, has been constantly torn between natural love of child and loyalty to husband. Things aren't improved by Caroline having a younger brother who Frank, the father, dotes on. The boy can do no wrong; Caro can do no right. Impossible situation. I live near them, live alone, and' – he lowered his head – 'Caroline often came to see me when she was unhappy. I gave her undivided affection and attention. We've always been very close. She's even confided about her love affairs; her first schoolgirl crush.' He lifted his head and looked Samson straight in the eyes. 'I expect all this sounds damn silly to you.'

'Not in the least. I'm fairly familiar at second-hand with the more depressing side of family life.'

'Um.' Camber cleared his throat. 'Now for point four. Events leading up to Caroline's abduction. Have you ever heard of Eventide Joy, Mr Samson? Or a man who goes by the name of Irving O?'

'No.'

'Nor had I a few days ago. It's one of these damn pseudo-religious cults that are springing up all over the place, usually started by some damn foreigner. Money is the objective and the means of getting money is to inflict religious hocus-pocus on easily-led, confused and disturbed young people. Caroline got caught up in the web. Won't go into details. Not too sure, to be honest. But I'm deeply suspicious of this particular cult. It seems the kids are trained to bring comfort to lonely old people and when I say comfort I mean sex among other things. The old people shell out their savings, and alter their wills in favour of Eventide Joy, out of sheer gratitude. This, plus a skilled team with collecting boxes, brings in a fair income. I have reason to believe the kids go through a sort of brainwashing conversion before they're let loose, but hard evidence is difficult to find.

'Anyway, to cut a long story short, Caroline joined this mob. There was one painful visit home and then – nothing. Mabel was quite beside herself. Somehow she, or she and Frank, managed to trace her to a place in the West Country. Big house with high wire fences and Alsatian guard dogs. Headquarters of this Irving O. The next bit makes me sound a bloody fool. Well, I was a bloody fool. I won't deny it. I played along. I agreed to go down to Tewkesbury and hang around in a hotel until I got the tip that she was in town. I was to intercept her and plead with her to come home. They said I was the only one who could work the trick. Caro trusted me, you see.

'What I didn't know was that Frank had hired two thugs called "deprogramming technicians" to kidnap her once I'd got her alone. The long and short of it is that she was kidnapped from right under my nose in broad daylight. Ashamed to admit that in spite of all my training I was rooted to the spot. She was hustled into a van and driven away before I could say Jack Robinson.' He felt in his pocket, produced his spectacles once more, and read from a slip of paper. 'I got the van number. Here.' He handed Samson the paper.

'And you want me to trace ownership of the van in the hope that this will lead to Caroline's captors?'

The colonel nodded vigorously. 'You've got it in one. Fact is, when I returned empty-handed and with a few pointed questions to ask, there was one hell of a quarrel. Haven't been on speaking terms with Frank or my daughter since. Seems they paid these so-called technicians to re-

13

convert Caroline, to wipe out the effects of the religious brainwashing. In my opinion that's every bit as immoral as the original brainwashing. Two wrongs never make a right.'

Samson stroked his chins. 'I've never been entirely convinced by that proposition. So much depends on relativity. But we won't argue about it now. How long is it since Caroline was abducted?'

'Two days ago. I just can't get any information about her except that she's still "undergoing treatment". Doesn't that phrase strike a chill in you? It does in me.'

Samson gazed at one of his favourite clocks before replying. Its mechanism had been still at ten minutes past twelve and on its face were large roman numerals in the centre of which, inside tiny circles, were the arabic equivalents. For him the clock was a reminder that too much explanation sometimes obscured what was being explained. At the moment, however, no explanations needed to be made, but there were important matters to be settled clearly and concisely.

'I'll take the case on,' he said, 'but I must tell you that my fees are fairly steep.'

'Money is no object, Mr Samson. No price is too high to pay for Caroline's recovery.'

'Even a hundred pounds a day plus expenses?'

Camber swallowed. 'So be it.'

Samson gave a slight smile. 'Don't worry. It won't be as much as that. Thirty at the most and then only if I spend the whole day on it. I'll keep expenses to a minimum.'

'Good chap. I'm not a rich man.'

'I think I should tell you that I've recorded everything

you've said. I'll play the tape back and stop it at the places where I want supplementary information. All right?'

'Yes, if that's the way to get results.'

Samson leaned forward, resting his elbows on the desk. 'I can promise results, but whether the results will be to your liking is something I can't guarantee.'

'Fair enough.' Camber began polishing his spectacles with a handkerchief which he extracted from the breast pocket of his coat. This operation gave him a reason for not looking at Samson while he was speaking.

'I expect I must strike you as something of a stereotype. A blimp.'

'I never judge a person on the image presented.'

'No. Quite. But I can't expect you to understand why this is so important to me, why money isn't any object, and why I'm prepared for it to blow up in my face. It isn't just that I love Caroline, although that's part of it.' He hesitated and polished the clean lenses even more furiously. 'Fact is,' he began, and then dried up.

When there was no sign that he was going to continue Samson filled in the silence. 'Would the fact be that you feel you've let Caroline down? You feel that you were the only one she really trusted and now she may think you abused that trust by leading her into the hands of these technicians?'

Camber put away his shining glasses. 'Absolutely spot on. By Jove, I think we're going to get somewhere. To be honest, when I first came in . . .'

'You weren't very impressed.'

'I wasn't going to say . . .'

'Of course not. And now I'll play back the tape.'

When Camber had gone, Samson summoned Shandy. He

outlined the problem and asked if she could recall reading about Irving O in any newspaper or magazine.

'Not a thing,' she said, 'but I do remember seeing something in *Time Out* about deprogramming. It sounds very nasty. There's someone in America who claims to have freed at least a thousand kids from the clutches of religious cults. But some of the methods used are pretty brutal.'

Samson nodded. 'There was an article in *The Times* about it too. An organisation has been set up in London which offers to train people in brainwashing techniques. The article ran to three or four columns and mentioned that the Yard's Special Branch were keeping an eye on the organisation. I think I'll have a word with Bernard. Can you get him on the line for me?'

When Samson had first taken over the run-down debt collecting agency which had belonged to his uncle and was beginning to expand the side which dealt with private enquiries he received some advice from an elderly lawyer who had given him more business than any other client. 'Always keep on the right side of the police,' the lawyer had said. 'Help them when you can and, if you get their trust, they will help you. Don't trespass on their territory. Contribute to the Police Benevolent Fund. In the long run you'll get better dividends than those private eyes who try to beat the police at their own job.'

Samson had generally followed this advice and now had contacts with the local police and in New Scotland Yard. Bernard was such a contact. Samson asked him what he knew about deprogramming.

'Don't tell me you've got a case of it,' said Bernard.

'I might have.'

'We'd be very glad to have some firm evidence if you get any. We know it goes on in America. There are supposed to be about three hundred trained deprogrammers over there. And we suspect it's started in England but unless we get a complaint what can we do? The cults don't complain, they've got too much to hide. The parents don't complain; they know they've acted improperly, if not illegally, in having their child kidnapped. And the victim doesn't complain. He or she is "cured" and so what is there to complain about? Although I know of one case in America where a young member of the Hare Krishna sect brought a prosecution against a man who had tried to deprogramme him and the fellow was sentenced to a year in jail.'

'I've read about an organisation in London which reckons to train deprogrammers. Can you tell me anything about it?'

'Not a lot,' replied Bernard. 'It got a spate of adverse publicity. *The Guardian*, *The Times*, and other papers ran stories on it, to say nothing of journals like *Psychology Today* and *The New Humanist*. Things suddenly went very quiet.'

'Can you give me any leads on who might be actively engaged in this sort of brainwashing? Where does the word "deprogramming" come from, anyway? It's not in my dictionary.'

'No leads at all. As for the word, I believe it was coined by the man who pioneered the method, an American called Ted Patrick. He invented the word about five years ago.'

'The treatment used can be brutal, I believe.'

'It certainly can,' said Bernard. 'Sensory deprivation techniques are used, victims are often stripped naked and may be physically assaulted. Beaten. Thrown into the air and allowed to fall to the ground. That sort of thing.'

'And parents let this happen?' There was a note, not

of disbelief, but of sadness for the human race in Samson's voice.

Bernard paused before replying. 'It's easy to be critical,' he said, 'but some parents get quite frantic when they see the child they love become a religious zombie. Any means justify the ends of recovering their normality. Or that's how they see it.'

'Means justifying the ends has been the excuse of every warmonger, torturer and sadist in history, to say nothing of terrorists and militant revolutionaries,' remarked Samson. 'But let's not get into philosophy. Thanks, Bernard. I'm very grateful. If I can get any firm evidence, and it won't damage my client's interests, you can be sure I'll get in touch again.'

CHAPTER TWO

Shandy almost slipped on the damp flagstones outside the church. She was steadied by the curate who took her arm. 'Careful,' he said. 'Now then. What did you want to know?'

'Whether you could tell me anything about a man called Stephen Hungerford.'

The curate was a young man with curly red hair and sparkling green eyes. 'What a question to ask in the pouring rain,' he said. 'You'd better come inside.'

He folded the umbrella he had been holding and led her into the church. She noticed a change of smell from the mellow faintly resinous scent of aged wood to that of well-worn vestments in which was trapped the personal odours of male choristers and servers. Rows of cassocks and surplices hung against one wall and she saw, propped against the opposite wall, a couple of electric guitars.

He observed her looking at the guitars. 'I'm one of those trendy priests,' he said. 'I like cheerful worship. Please sit down.' He indicated a chair beside a long highly-polished table made of elm wood. 'What is your name?'

'Elaine. Elaine Bullivant. My boss calls me Shandy.'

'I thought shandy was out of fashion as a drink. You don't look out of fashion.'

'My boss isn't a very fashionable sort of man although he's up to date on modern technology.' She glanced through leaded-light windows at the rain. 'If there was another Flood he's more likely to build a spaceship than an ark.'

The curate smiled. 'What does he do for a living?'

Shandy decided to play it absolutely straight. 'He's a private detective,' she said, 'and he's been engaged to find a girl who's been abducted.'

A curiously puzzled look came to the curate's face. 'That doesn't sound like Stephen. Where does he fit in?'

Shandy outlined Camber's story of how Caroline had been snatched and driven away in a van. The van's registration number had led to Stephen Hungerford but unfortunately he had changed his address and no one knew where he could be found. However, a former neighbour had provided the information that he had taken a degree in theology at Cambridge University. On her own initiative (her boss knew nothing of this) she had found out the names of graduates in Stephen's year in the hope that she might find someone who lived close, someone who might be willing to talk to her and throw light on Stephen's character and give a lead as to where he might be now. 'It was a hell of a search,' she said, 'and I've run up an astronomical telephone bill but I finally came up with you. Sonning isn't a very usual name and I found out from *Crockford's Clerical Directory* there was a Reverend Charles Sonning in a parish less than three miles from our office. It was a long shot,' she concluded, 'I hope it's going to pay off.' She looked searchingly into his eyes.

'But why should Stephen want to kidnap a girl? It doesn't fit with what I remember of him.'

She explained what Camber had told Samson about deprogramming.

The curate's cheerful mien hardened into disapproval. 'I'm glad you found me. So much persistence deserves a reward. But I'm afraid I can't help much. I was at the same college as Stephen but we didn't have much in common.' He paused. 'He wasn't the easiest person to get along with.'

'Why was that?'

'Well, this isn't going to be easy to put across.' He looked slightly embarrassed as he spoke. 'You see, Stephen had strong likes and dislikes and one of his dislikes – it was almost obsessional – was a dislike of homosexuals. He was what is known as a queer-basher. It nearly got him sent down twice and on one occasion he ended up in hospital with a broken nose. The basher had been bashed.'

'He went out looking for homosexuals to pick a fight with?'

'More or less. There was no shortage of talent. Coteries exist at every university. But paradoxically his only real friend at college was an extremely comely young man. I'm not suggesting that Stephen and this young student of divinity had anything but a platonic relationship, but this fellow's suicide, shortly after having joined some esoteric sect, completely shattered Stephen.' The curate paused. 'I never expected Stephen would take holy orders. And I never dreamed he would declare war on these religious sub-cults. Although perhaps I should have known. A couple of years or so ago I saw a book reviewed in *The Church Times*. The title was something like *Massacre of the Innocents*. No, it was *Manipulation of the Innocent*. I noticed Stephen was the author. But apart from that I'm afraid I can't tell you anything. I've no idea where he may be now although in the back of my mind I seem to remember his family home was somewhere in East Anglia.'

'Thanks. You've given me something to work on.'

As Shandy stood up the curate also rose to his feet.

'No need for you to go all the way down the church,' he said. 'I can let you out of a side door.'

'I'm sorry if I've delayed you at all.'

'It's been a pleasure . . . When are you expecting your baby to arrive?'

She gave a rueful laugh. 'You're more observant than my boss.'

'Bosses never see things they don't wish to see.' He led the way to the door. 'Do you belong to the Church of England?'

'I've rather lapsed,' she replied sheepishly. 'That is, I used to go as a child, and I got married in church, but I never go these days.'

He opened the door. It was still raining heavily and the gravestones in a small adjacent burial ground had a wet sheen.

'If you should want your baby baptised here I should be most happy to oblige.' He held out his hand.

'Thanks. I might take you up on that.'

'And be careful how you go. These flagstones are terribly slippery. We don't want you falling.'

She caressed her stomach. 'I've fallen already.'

He laughed. She noticed that he didn't close the door until she was safely in the street.

Samson lived in a flat about a mile from his office. It was on the first floor of a house which had a façade blotched by peeling stucco. On each side of the house were buildings boarded up against vandalism. The street was part of an area of urban decay which rain never refreshed and sunlight could not brighten. He didn't care for the district and was searching for a more permanent home where he could accommodate his collection of clocks. In the meanwhile, he spent more time than necessary in his office. The flat was nothing more than a place where he could sleep, wash and have his breakfast. Recently he had flirted with the idea of trying to find a place in the West End and commuting each day to his office in south-east London, but the news of Shandy's pregnancy had obliged him to shelve this plan. When she left he would need to spend more time than ever in the office.

When she hadn't appeared by nine Samson felt a twinge of apprehension. She was always punctual and on the rare occasions when she was likely to be late she would telephone. He opened the morning mail, standing in her room and glancing from time to time out of the window to the street below. Rain was falling steadily and every pedestrian seemed to be hurrying. Road traffic was dense; it was the rush-hour; and the impatience of some drivers with the weather, and the slow crawl into the City, was blasted out by honking horns.

Nine-fifteen. He decided to go to his room and finish a report he had to make on pilfering at a light industrial plant together with a recommendation for future security. For a while he forgot Shandy. The document was not easy to draft because he had been instructed to make it low-key. It must contain nothing which could be used by the union to cause disruption of work on the shop-floor. The phrase 'articles removed without authority' had to be inserted in place of 'stolen goods', and management criticised for placing temptation in the path of decent, honest workers.

It was ten-forty by the time he had finished the piece of hypocritical double-think and he was becoming very worried about Shandy. He decided to call her home number. There was no reply. Presumably her husband had gone to work as usual, but where was she?

23

An incidental drawback of her late arrival was that he was accustomed to having coffee and two or three dough-nuts between ten-fifteen and ten-thirty, and it was she who brought them, fresh from a baker's shop, on her way to the office. He walked to the window. Rain was still hatched against the buildings opposite but its slats were wider spaced and the sky seemed lighter. Below, the street surface glistened and umbrellas bobbed and weaved. A coloured youth, wearing T-shirt and jeans, was pushing a pram filled with flowers and holding a dainty yellow parasol over it. And then Samson saw her, scuttling through a gap between two buses.

She arrived out of breath. 'Sorry I'm late,' she said, taking off a pink rainproof and hanging it behind the door.

'I've been dreadfully worried,' he began.

'Worried about this,' she asked, placing a confectionery box on the table.

'Worried about you. Where have you been?'

'Tell you in a minute. I'll put on the coffee.'

She went to a small annexe where there was a sink, an electric plug and an electric ring.

He followed and stood behind her. 'I saw you cross the road. In your condition you really must take more care.'

'Don't fuss, Samson. Open the goodies and see what you've got this morning.'

He prised open the box and saw his mid-morning snack, three large buns bursting with cream and oozing strawberry jam.

'Aha! This is a guilt offering, is it? Something to make up for being so late?'

She came out of the annexe and flicked back her hair. 'Sort of. But I've been working on a case.'

'What case? Not that boring Silhouette case?'

'No. Although you might say it involves a silhouette. The silhouette of Stephen Hungerford. I've been trying to make him more three-dimensional.'

Samson selected a bun and, exercising delicate skill acquired by long practice, managed to take a mouthful without losing any cream. As he masticated and took further cautious bites she told him of her encounter with the curate. 'And so,' she concluded, 'we now know he is aggressively anti-homosexual which probably means he is a latent homosexual, and we know he is the author of a book called *Manipulation of the Innocent*.'

She awaited Samson's reaction.

The gentle sob of percolating coffee came from the annexe.

'These are good buns,' he said at last.

'In other words, you reckon I've wasted my time. And please don't tell me that nobody "wastes time" but Time wastes us all.'

'I was going to have said that. But there is a school of thought which believes that if you enjoy wasting time then the time you've enjoyed wasting isn't wasted time. The motto of this school is *dolce far niente*.'

'Have I wasted my time?'

'No. You've got a man ready and willing to baptise your baby.'

'That does it,' she said. 'I'll show you who's the detective around here.'

Having polished off the first bun Samson was looking tenderly at the second, but the tone of her voice interrupted his contemplation. 'What do you mean?'

'I'm going to track down this book, read it and see if I can learn anything more about Mr Hungerford.'

'You're not to over-exert yourself.'

She laughed incredulously. 'Thank God my husband isn't like you.'

Samson contrived to look hurt while licking a smear of jam from his finger.

'I know it's well meant,' she said, 'but let me carry on as usual.'

A twinkle came to his eyes. 'Locate Stephen Hungerford for me and I'll give you an extra week's pay as a bonus.'

'Done,' she replied promptly.

After a day of incessant rain it was mild and sunny; a steady drone of traffic came from the street below and not a single car-horn was banged in anger. People complained about the climate but Samson enjoyed the unpredictability of English weather. He had once explained to Shandy when she had spoken longingly of islands in the sun that there is no stimulus in guaranteed sunshine and human beings need stimulus. It had been the stimulus of foul weather which had caused barbarian hordes in ancient times to overrun civilisation. She had given a faint smile of disbelief at this conjecture.

He was thinking about her love of the sun and wondering whether her baby would be mercilessly exposed to its rays next summer when she walked in.

'Well,' he asked.

'I think I know the area where you can find Stephen Hungerford.'

Although he had promised Colonel Camber that there would be results, Samson had not hurried himself to obtain any. There were certain types of case, particularly those which were inspired by bitter hatred between marriage partners, which resolved themselves. You could spend laborious hours sniffing out evidence of adultery only to find, when you presented the facts, either that there had been confession and reconciliation or (an increasingly fashionable solution) that a *menage à trois* had been set up. You found yourself unwanted, an unwelcome spectre at a love-feast, and you were quickly paid off.

Samson's hunches weren't often wrong but he had the hunch that by the time Stephen Hungerford was found the errant Caroline would be reunited with her family, Camber would say something like 'Feel like a man with egg on my face. What?' and the file would be closed. This was his hunch and yet – he couldn't quite put a finger on it – he sensed the case might snake off in a totally different direction.

He gave her a benign smile. 'Where can I find Hungerford?'

'In fenland. Possibly somewhere near a village called Fen Soken.' From behind her back she produced a book and handed it to Samson.

He turned the slim volume over. 'An enquiry into the techniques used by practitioners of some fringe religions,' he read aloud.

'Look inside the dust-jacket. At the back.'

Samson opened the book and his eyes scanned a biographical note headed 'About the Author'.

Stephen Hungerford was born at Fen Soken, a village in the heart of East Anglia. He was educated at the village school and later at a grammar school in Cambridgeshire. After taking a degree in theology he was fortunate in securing a grant from a major foundation to enable him to make a sociological analysis of the Japanese Soka Gakkai movement, Christian Science and the Divine Light Mission. During the research he became interested in 'manipulationist' sects and this book is a result of that interest. Although he lives in south London he is at present converting a derelict cottage not far from his native village. Eventually he hopes to use this as a base for a comprehensive investigation into fenland culture, a subject which to date has escaped the attention of sociologists and anthropologists alike.

Samson put down the book. 'Have you read it?'

'Yes. It's an odd mixture of prejudice and scientific jargon. He doesn't call them sects or cults, they are "deviant belief systems".'

'Any insights into the author's character?'

'Some, but I haven't sorted them out yet. I'd have to read it again. He tries to sound reasonable and detached but emotive adjectives keep popping in. I'd guess he was impulsive and an obsessive.'

Samson turned in his swivel chair and faced the shelves of books behind his desk. These were crammed with directories and other reference works. They were in no special order; some lay on their sides; others had been replaced upside down. *Who's Who* was edged between *International Dictionary of Sign Language* and *Black's Medical Dictionary*, but Samson knew exactly where to find whatever he wanted and his hand went unerringly to a road atlas of Great Britain. He flicked through its pages.

'As I thought,' he said gloomily. 'The fens cover a wide area.'

'But Fen Soken pinpoints the part to search.'

'If he's taken her to the derelict cottage. We haven't a shred of evidence that he went there in the van.'

'It's a start,' she persisted. 'And there will be people who know him and may have ideas where to find him.'

Samson stroked his chins, tipped his head on one side and regarded her with a very curious look.

'Why are you looking at me like that,' she demanded. 'You're taking an exceptional interest in this case. Why?'

'I'm on to a bonus.'

He shook his head. 'I think you identify with the girl. You want to help her.'

'For heaven's sake, Samson! You ought to know by now that I never get emotionally involved with my work.'

'Don't you?'

'Never. My emotions are committed elsewhere.'

He replaced the road atlas and faced her again. 'I was wondering,' he said, 'how you'd feel about becoming a business partner. A junior partner.'

It was her turn to give a curious look. 'What's the catch,' she asked.

'No catch. I'm impressed with the progress you've made on this unpromising case.'

'I've done as well on others and there's never been a whisper about partnerships.'

'Just an idea.'

Comprehension flooded her face. She threw back her head and laughed. 'I get it!'

'Get what?'

'Make me a partner at a salary something like I'm getting now and I shan't be an employee any more. And you won't have to give me maternity pay.'

He looked affronted. 'Nothing of the sort. The thought never passed my mind.'

'If it didn't, then I can only think you must be slipping.' She picked up the book. 'I'll think about it.'

The genesis of a smile crinkled his upper lip. 'You won't regret it.'

'But . . . will you?' she retorted as she left the room.

A few minutes later she buzzed him.

'Yes?'

'Developments,' she said. 'I've got Camber on the line. He wants to see you urgently.'

'Put him through and listen in.'

The voice was instantly recognisable. 'That you, Samson?'

'Speaking.'

'Must see you. Situation quite out of hand. When can I come?'

Samson glanced at his watch. 'In an hour?'

'Right.'

'Can you give me an idea of what's happened?'

'Caroline's life in real danger. Explain all when I see you. It's become a different ball game, as our American friends say. See you in an hour.'

CHAPTER THREE

She had a remote expression in her eyes as though she were looking through the two men who confronted her and through a thick cottage wall to a place far beyond the flat horizon. Although the three of them were sitting so close that their knees almost touched, her distant look was only a part of a veil of detachment which covered her as materially as the long faded ethnic dress she wore. The men waited for an answer. They had limitless time available; they could afford to wait.

The taller of the men, young, and with a smoothly angelic face in spite of a nose which had been broken more than once, gave a gentle prompting. 'Well, Caroline?'

She gazed blankly as though her thoughts were fixed to some far galaxy in the night sky.

The young man wore jeans and an open-neck shirt under a khaki bomber jacket; he had a degree in theology, was an expert on fringe religions and was greatly interested in fenland culture. His partner, darker and older, with balding scalp and heavy eyebrows, was a psychologist who in the debate between psychotherapists and behaviourists had finally come down on the side of behaviourism while conceding that there was room for some Freudian and post-Freudian theories, particularly those which involved transactional analysis.

'Well, Caroline?'

She opened her mouth but didn't speak.

'When you went to live with Irving did you know that he had been convicted in the United States for corrupting minors, that he's spent five years in mental institutions, and that he has at least a million dollars in his own name in a Swiss bank account and real estates in France and Canada? Did you know that?'

At last she spoke and it was as though she was echoing a platitude which long ago had become a ripple of meaningless syllables. 'Love is God and God is love,' she said.

'I believe that God is God,' replied the fair-haired man, 'and I know that many good people believe that God is love, but please explain to me how love is God. Or do you mean lust is God. Because I can accept *that* as a belief. It's sure enough the belief of people like Irving O. But how can love be God, Caroline?'

She gazed at and through him and said nothing. Her hands lay folded like a bird at rest on her lap.

'I know I'm a stranger, but I want to be a friend. And I know what we did to get you here was sneaky. But it was less sneaky than what Irving did to get you into that fortress of his.' He inched his chair forward so that his face was close to hers. It was part of his skill as a technician to apply the crowding technique to make the subject feel physically oppressed. 'Did you know, by the way,' he continued, 'that Irving has to pay a terrific premium on his insurance?'

Her lack of response was total; she might have been deaf and dumb.

'He's insured himself against accident or disabling illness and the premium is so high because of the number of times he's been treated for venereal disease. Did you know that, Caroline?'

She gazed towards a space that was beyond Arcturus.

'I'm not lying. I have a photo-copy of his medical report. I'll show it you later. He's had it all: gonorrhoea, syphilis, the lot.'

The other man thrust his neck forward. He too was crowding the girl, not with a verbal barrage but with the force of his silence.

'Caroline,' said the fair-haired man, 'I'm speaking to you. Did you know about Irving's record of VD?'

'Love is God and God is love,' she replied.

'You mean God loves sinners and pardons them?'

'God is love and love is God.'

The fair-haired man smiled. 'Hold it, Caroline. You reversed the order there. You put "God is love" first. Until now it's been "Love is God" first. Why did you reverse the order?'

Her eyelids flickered and she began twisting her hands; the bird at rest on her lap had become a bird to be strangled.

'I can see you've had enough, Caroline. If I belonged to the secret police I'd increase the pressure. Or if I was an expert in brainwashing, like Irving, I'd do the same. But I'm not. I'm an ordinary human being doing his best to help. You want help, don't you?'

'Love is God and God is love.'

'So you say. But repeating a *mantra* isn't going to help. I know Irving told you to say it whenever you were in a tight spot, but you're not in a tight spot now. You're free. Would you like to leave? To walk out?'

Something about the girl changed. Her air of detachment was diminished, but she said nothing.

33

'Would you like to leave, Caroline? Walk out of here and into the night? Would you?'

'Yes.'

It was the first time she had spoken to him instead of at him.

'Very well. You shall.' He stood up. 'Come with me.'

Rather shakily, as though she had become numbed by inactivity, she rose to her feet.

'I must blindfold you,' he said. 'It wouldn't be fair on us if you knew where we lived. So I'll lead you away from the house and when we're well clear you'll be on your own. You can take off the blindfold and go wherever you want. You can go back to Irving if he means so much to you. He'll punish you for disobedience but you won't mind that. A poor disorientated kid like you welcomes punishment. It makes you feel square with yourself. Right?'

She shook her head.

'You won't feel square with yourself?'

'Let me go,' she said.

'Okay. Come along.'

When they had gone the other man stood up and shook his head in a belated gesture of disapproval. After lighting a cigarette he went to the largest, best-furnished room in the cottage where he poured a whisky, sat down, and reached for a folder of papers marked 'C.M..'

Although the room was equipped with hi-fi stereo and television for entertainment, and deep leather armchairs for relaxation, it had the transient look of a stage set or an airport lounge. It was not a place where the history of human lives was subtly recorded by the gradual accretion of objects having special associations so much as an anonymous instant backdrop for travelling players. And the man, even with thick eyebrows and sparse hair to distinguish him, looked like an identikit picture of the average man. In his grey suit, walking down a half-empty street, nobody would have given him a second glance. He looked like any sombre, down-in-the-mouth office commuter travelling early to dodge the rush-hour. Even his name, James Brown, was unremarkable.

He read through the papers which were filled with biographical details of Caroline's life. At the point where it said 'She has a morbid fear of drowning' he put the file aside and went to the record-player. In spite of his appearance and his commitment to behavioural psychology he wasn't without a romantic streak. He liked sad music and unhappy endings. After carefully dusting the disc he placed an excerpt from *Tristan and Isolde* on the turntable.

She had travelled in the back of a closed van and had no idea of where she had been taken, and now she was being led by the hand into the night. The air was chilly and had the dampness of rising mist. Underfoot the ground was soft and spongy and she guessed she was being guided across a field.

She heard the sound of an aeroplane passing high overhead and for a wild moment wondered if Irving had come to rescue her in his private helicopter, but the sound faded and she could hear nothing but the slight swish of her dress as it brushed against tall grass.

She tried to concentrate her thoughts on Irving. He had taught her that if she centred her mind on the letter O, and repeated O incessantly to herself, she would establish a telepathic link with him. But after a few Os her concentration was broken by stumbling over a tussock. Her companion saved her from falling and dragged her forward once more. Weak from a long period of undernourishment, and exhausted by the effort of resisting questioning, she felt a strong desire to wrench herself free so that she could lie down and go to sleep. But he kept pulling her along; she was a prisoner being forcibly escorted to freedom.

'Nearly there,' he said.

Before she could stop herself she asked, 'Where?'

'To where we say good-bye. It's been nice knowing you, Caroline. I'd like to have helped, but you didn't want my help.'

The ground seemed softer and her shoes made squelching noises. She was aware that her feet were cold and wet. He stopped and she bumped against him.

'Count to ten slowly and then take off your blindfold. There's a road about half a mile ahead of you. It's up to you what you do when you reach it but if you've got any sense you'll try to make it to your parents' home. They love you and want you back. But, as I say, it's up to you. Good-bye.'

She counted and then tore off the scarf which bandaged her eyes. The moon was in its last quarter and the stars looked like flecks of bright paint sprayed from a gigantic atomiser. It was beautifully clear above, but from below her shoulders the ground was covered in swathes of mist. She turned slowly around. The mist spread in all directions and there wasn't a sign of any sort of life. The man had completely vanished.

He had said a road was half a mile ahead but because she had turned she wasn't sure where 'ahead' lay. She began to feel frightened. 'Help me, Irving,' she whispered, and her mind pictured vividly his face, sloe-black eyes and fringe of white hair. 'Come to me, my child,' he seemed to say, 'and be born again.'

'Where are you?'

'Think of the word "God". What is the middle letter? Think of the divine O. O is the essence of God. I am O. Come to me.'

'Where are you?' she cried aloud, and began to stumble forward, but with every step she seemed to become more tired and weak. It was difficult to put one leg in front of the other and she was conscious that the cold wetness of her feet was creeping up past her ankles. It seemed that she was in a swamp where pools of water lay around hummocks of sedge.

The effort of dragging her feet through mire which gave noisy sucks at every step left her panting for breath. She forgot Irving and that love was God as panic swept over her. 'Help,' she screamed, but the scream came out as a whisper. 'Help,' she yelled, but it was so faint that she could hardly hear it herself. Panic became absolute. It was as though every fearful emotion was raging through every nerve of her body and reason was something so extinct that it could never have existed except as an illusion.

She blundered through the mist and deeper into a marsh where reeds and rushes brushed their tall tips against her flailing hands. The rank odour of marsh mud, decaying vegetable matter and stagnant water seemed to clog her nostrils. It was becoming difficult to breathe.

'Get a grip on yourself,' said a voice in her head, but it wasn't Irving's voice. It was her father's.

And then she realised she was nearly up to her knees in soft mud and unable to move. 'Help,' she screamed, and this time her voice rang through the marshes. 'Help! Help! Help!'

A distant owl on a hunting expedition from a fenland barn gave an answering derisive screech.

'Help!'

If I stay still, she thought, I shan't sink. I must stay like this. How long till daylight? The men had taken her wrist-watch as soon as they entered the cottage. This had confirmed her belief in Irving. He had warned her, and the other girl acolytes, that if unscrupulous relatives, motivated by self-interest and bourgeois attitudes, tried to abduct them and put them in the hands of therapists, or, worse, deprogramming technicians, they must expect to lose personal possessions. And if sensory deprivation techniques were to be used they would be left without means of telling the time and might have to endure weeks of being locked in a cupboard and made to eat their food like a dog from a dish on the floor. They would be degraded and humiliated.

Irving's punishments for bad thinking were designed to strengthen their resistance to deprogramming. It wasn't cruelty that made him order them lick the floor wherever he walked. He did it from a sense of protective love. It was for their own good.

He had told them of all the perverted and disgusting tricks deprogrammers used. 'They won't let you wash,' he had said, 'and when you go to the toilet they will stand beside you. You will be made to wipe yourself with paper that has a likeness of my face printed on it. Don't refuse. Do as they say. You have a remedy. You can detach yourselves with your own personal keyword and for your inquisitors you simply repeat your personal *mantra* over and over again. If you do this they will never break you.'

The memory of Irving's assurances was a comfort but it was short-lived. The wet-cold was encroaching up her thighs. She was sinking.

With a tremendous effort she dragged her right leg slightly forward.

As a child she had once freed a fly from a spider's web

38

but her father, who had seen her, had said, 'That's a stupid thing to do. Flies spread diseases. Spiders are there to keep flies down. Do you want a world infested with flies?' She had been unable to answer, choked by the sense of unworthiness and guilt which her father always seemed to induce. It was only when she was in her late teens that she'd realised that she had identified with the fly and this was why she had wanted to release it. And because of the identification she had superstitiously thought: If I do this for the fly, some day someone will do the same for me. It was time for the fly's debt to be repaid.

'Help,' she called.

Oh God, I'm going to drown!

'Help!' It was a wail of despair.

Stinking mud. Smells worse than shit. I'm too young to die. Drowning. Didn't I beat it once before?

'Help!'

Christ Jesus God . . . O . . . O . . . O . . . O . . . O . . . O

'Help.' It was a whisper again. Her lungs seemed full of mist and mud. Dying. Daddy, where are you?

'Hold this,' said a voice out of the mist and she felt something hard against her stomach. 'Hold tight,' said the voice which she now recognised as belonging to the fair-haired man. 'I'll pull you out.'

Her life depended on her grip and she held the wooden pole like a steel clamp.

When she was on firmer ground an outline materialised. 'It's me. Stephen.'

'I know who it is.'

He took her hand. 'I'll take you back,' he said. 'You're obviously not ready yet to go out on your own. Follow close and don't let go.'

She didn't speak until the cottage lights were in sight.

'You set this up,' she spat. 'You bastard deprogrammer!'
'That's a big word for a little girl.'
'Don't try to patronise me.'
'Wouldn't dream of it.'
'I hate you!'
'Good. That's fine. I like it.'
They entered the front porch.
'I'll take you to your room,' he said.
'I'd like a wash.'
'Sorry. No can do.'
They were now inside the cottage. Her eyes blazed at him. 'You don't surprise me,' she said. 'Water for washing isn't allowed on deprogramming, is it?'
'I don't get this deprogramming business. What's it mean? Deprogramming?'
'No water for hygiene.'
The fair-haired man smiled. 'Irving has briefed you well about something. I don't know what, but he's briefed you about something. What is deprogramming?'
'Love is God and God is love.'
'No. We're not back to square one, however much you may wish it. We're firmly on square two.' He opened the door of her room. 'Don't go to sleep. I'm going to get you something to eat.' He looked her up and down. 'Hey, what's happened to your shoes?'
She made no reply.
'Lose them in the mud, did you? Never mind, it won't harm you to be barefoot.'

CHAPTER FOUR

The kitchen was filled with appliances in gleaming chrome and white enamel. Apart from the walls, tiled in pale green, and the cupboards in light oak laminate, the place had the surgical look of an operating theatre. Electricity was supplied by a generator outside the cottage but water had never been laid on and had to be drawn from a well in the front yard. Because there was no main drainage waste went into a septic tank in the small back garden.

Having washed his hands Stephen opened the refrigerator and selected a piece of fillet steak. 'Can I do one for you while I'm about it,' he asked.

The other man shook his head. 'That was a dangerous chance and it was a mistake,' he said.

'It was perfectly safe.'

'We agreed to discuss when was the best time for inducing major disturbances, if necessary. You jumped the gun.'

'I played it by ear. It was a great opportunity to win confidence, and winning confidence is the name of the game. And it may have worked. If fear can wipe clean what you call the "cortical slate", then hers should be whiter than white.' He grinned. 'She was in a blue funk which gave the cleaning that extra blue-whiteness.'

'We agreed to discuss strategy step by step. We did not agree to unilateral play-it-by-ear exercises.'

Stephen took a bottle of Worcester sauce and sprinkled it on the steak. 'This is how she likes it, according to her mother. It'll be interesting to see how she responds to what was her favourite dish before she got on to that low-protein diet of Irving's.'

Brown's eyebrows converged like rival caterpillars. It was the only sign that he felt anger. His face remained impassive as any well-scrubbed potato which the caterpillars might have chosen to crawl over. 'Don't change the subject,' he said calmly. 'We did not agree that you should play anything by ear. This is a scientific exercise, not a test of your aural virtuosity.'

'It did no harm. Could have made a breakthrough.'

'But it hasn't. I heard what she was saying to you. She was angry and talking about deprogramming and then she went back to that stupid *mantra*. All you've done, my ear-playing friend, is to reinforce her present behaviour patterns. Skinner couldn't have done better with one of his rats.'

Stephen tipped broccoli heads into a saucepan and took a chip-basket from a cupboard. He spoke in short phrases between various actions. 'Let's get this straight. I'm in charge. You're my adviser. I lined this up. It's my show. The fact that she showed anger is a big step forward. Fear made her cry for help and anger made her sore with me after she'd been saved. She has shown two fundamental emotions. Before then it was a blank wall. I did the right thing and it was safe.'

'And what's the self-delusory rationalisation,' asked Brown in a voice that matched the heaviness of his frame. 'That you know the district like the back of your hand?'

'It's no delusion. I was born near here. And where I took her is one of the few pieces of unreclaimed fen. She was fairly close to dry land, and I was only a couple of paces behind her, crouching so that the mist covered me. It was safe.'

'Let me give you a word of warning.'

Stephen allowed a pile of chips to splash and sizzle in hot oil before saying, 'Go on.'

'Be on guard against an emotional transference.'

'Look. I may not know a cerebral cortex from a cerebellum, but I do know all about transference.'

'You sound like a man with a hot line to God. You know all about transference!' Brown laughed.

Stephen swung round. He no longer looked like a fresh-faced adult choirboy who, incidentally, had a broken nose, but a tough prizefighter. 'Leave God out of this,' he said. 'Okay?'

The other man stepped back as though avoiding an invisible fist. 'Okay,' he replied.

She dried herself in front of an electric fire but couldn't get rid of the dank smell of mud. She felt sickeningly unclean and longed for a bath of hot water and a bar of fragrant soap. Irving had been right. Self-disgust was something deprogrammers aimed to induce in their victims. He had helped to prepare her for just this sort of ordeal by his loving punishments, but perhaps the preparation hadn't been quite thorough enough. When he had ordered her to wear the filthy cast-off rags of a dead female tramp she had felt a curious exaltation. Now she simply felt dirty and degraded.

She looked round the room. Its window was boarded over and the door had a spy-hole set in one panel. The walls were of whitewashed brick and the only furnishings were a narrow single bed, a bare table, a tatty brown and yellow rug and a wheelback chair. A book entitled *Manipulation of the Innocent* lay on the table. A naked electric light bulb hung from the ceiling.

She went to the bed and lay down with her back to the door. Closing her eyes she concentrated on the memory of Irving's face but she was too tired to hold the image and her mind freewheeled into another picture and it was her father's face she saw.

For once he was paying attention to her. Usually she saw more of his profile than his full face and had often noticed that if he was in the room when she walked in he would look to see who had entered and then turn away. But if her younger brother came in unexpectedly he would smile and make some remark. However, in this memory he was looking straight at her. She had just spent a week in a London commune and had come home for the day to do her laundry. The family had finished a meal and her mother was pouring out coffee as he asked, 'And what exactly does this man Irving do for a living?'

'I've told you, Daddy. He's the Director of Eventide Joy.'

'Director? How very impressive!'

The irony in his voice was so abrasive that she was tempted to flare back, 'But you're a director too', but she smothered the retort.

'Let me get this straight,' he continued. 'You and the others in the commune work at ordinary jobs during the day, or queue up for the dole, and in your spare time you visit lonely old people in their homes. Is that a fair statement?'

44

She could feel herself growing tense. 'That's right.'

'And you've been visiting lonely old people this week?' Somehow he made it sound as though 'lonely old people' was a euphemism for worthless nonentities. She could see that the growing tension had reached her mother whose thin face had taken on a pinched look.

'It's something worth while,' she enthused desperately. 'Every night I've been reading *David Copperfield* to a poor blind old woman of eighty-seven who lives all by herself in a hovel of a bed-sit. You've no idea how grateful she was.'

'I expect she was terribly grateful,' said her mother quickly, as though trying to defuse an impending electric storm by murmuring soothing words into the wind.

'She gave me a sovereign. Of course I didn't want it, but she insisted. She got very upset when I refused. In the end I had to take it.'

Her father gave a low whistle. 'A sovereign. That was gratitude indeed. Have you brought it home to show us?'

Her brother who had been silent suddenly said, 'I'm going,' and left the room.

'Where's this famous sovereign,' asked her father.

'I handed it over. It belongs to Eventide Joy.'

His voice became icily precise. 'Correct me if I am wrong, but I thought it was a mere ninety per cent of your earnings, a trivial ninety per cent, that was collared by the man you call a director. He should have given you ten per cent of the value of the sovereign as your change. Did he?'

'I'd rather not discuss it,' she said, and was furious that her voice sounded breathless.

'Very well, we won't discuss it. The sovereign was yours

45

to do with as you wished. But tell me, how did a poor woman living in a hovel happen to have a sovereign?'

She could feel blood rushing to her face. She lowered her head.

Her mother pleaded, 'Must you, Frank? Can't we forget this wretched sovereign?'

'No, we can't. If you don't want to listen, take your coffee into the other room. I'll stay here with Caroline. I want to hear more about this peculiar outfit she's joined.'

Her mother gave a compassionate look but said nothing more. Her father continued, 'Tell me, I'm so ignorant about these things, but I thought in my ignorance that in a commune one shared everything. I never realised that ninety per cent of all you had was handed over to one person.'

She made a great effort to contain the rage boiling inside her. It was a fury she felt not only towards her father but also to her mother who was doing nothing to support her. At that moment she hated them both equally but keeping her voice calm she said, 'It's like this. It's called a commune but it is run by a committee. There has to be a committee to administer a charity. It's a legal and technical thing. The Director is employed by the committee.'

'I see. It's a registered charity, is it?'

'Eventide Joy is. The commune itself isn't.'

'Then I'm not sure I do see. But we won't argue about "legal and technical" things.' He reached for a bottle of brandy and for the first time his steadfast friendless gaze was diverted from her. 'I'd like to know what training you and the others get to prepare you for coping with all these poor lonely old people.'

'I do wish we could drop the subject,' intervened her mother in a last despairing cry into the wind.

46

She was ignored. The storm was exclusively between father and daughter. He was launching a frontal assault on the castle called Eventide Joy knowing that the last reserves of her self-esteem were protected by its walls.

She made a final attempt to call a truce. 'Irving has a house of his own in the country and every so often two or three of us go on a training course there. We learn how to cope with really difficult old folk, those who are senile but haven't yet been admitted to care by the authorities. I'm hoping to go there soon.'

'Whereabouts in the country?'

'Gloucestershire, I think.'

He didn't offer her a brandy; it was an omission she remembered later. Swirling his own in a balloon glass he asked, 'Would part of the training be directed towards ways and means of getting old people to alter their wills in favour of your Mr Irving – if that's his real name and not a crook's alias?'

Her anger welled out and she had blazed into a tirade of which she remembered nothing except the statues of her parents. Her mother was frozen in the act of lifting a cup of coffee and her father sat as though carved in rock.

Then she had raced from the house.

She heard her mother's plaintive cry, 'Your washing, Caroline,' against the sound of her own running footsteps.

This was the last time she had seen her parents.

As she recalled the scene, lying on a narrow bed, the hatred of her father burned like acid in her stomach. Having driven her from home by cold disdain and emotional neglect he was now trying to reclaim her and had used a dirty trick to trap her. As a special privilege she, and two other girls, had been allowed to visit a nearby town. They all had strict instructions not to separate. But while a man

47

had distracted the other two by grabbing their arms and saying, 'Have either of you lost a nightmare?', she, walking just behind them, had felt her hand taken. The others, confused by the odd question, hadn't seen her led away by the only man, apart from Irving, she trusted.

Her grandfather had taken her into an alleyway. 'Caro,' he had said, 'please come back. We're all worried stiff about you.'

'I can't, Grandad.'

Someone had seized her from behind, pinioning her arms, and she had been bundled into a waiting van at the end of the alley. She had glimpsed her grandfather looking bewildered and she heard him shout, 'Hey, wait a minute,' and then she was caged in the dark interior of the van and it was being driven out of town at speed.

The old man had been used as an agent for her capture but he was not guilty of deception. It was her father, she was certain, who had organised the snatch. He didn't want her, and yet he was too selfish to let anyone else have her; he was the dog that didn't want the hay in the manger and wouldn't allow any other animal to enter and eat it.

Exhausted, and feeling filthy with the stink of marsh mud in her nostrils, and torn between anger and self-pity, she began crying.

The door of her room opened.

'Feeling hungry,' asked Stephen. 'I've made something special for you.'

Surreptitiously she wiped her eyes with a corner of blanket and then rolled over.

He was carrying a tray which he placed carefully on the table.

'How about that?' he said with the pride of a satisfied cook. 'Smells good, doesn't it?'

'Get out and take that rubbish with you!'

For a moment he looked like a man who cannot believe he has been caught travelling with an out-of-date ticket. He stared incredulously at the tray. Steak glistened succulently in the centre of broccoli tips, chips and fried tomatoes. The ticket was all right. 'What do you mean? Rubbish?'

'I don't want it. I'm not eating until I've had a bath.'

'If you don't eat, you don't get anything for another twenty-four hours.'

'I'm not eating till I've had a bath.'

'Sorry. No deal.'

'I want a bath.'

'Sorry. No water. That's the rule. Anyway, I thought you weren't all that fond of water. Aren't you afraid of drowning if you had a bath?'

'Love is God and God is love.'

He smiled. 'See you. *Bon appétit.*'

As he moved towards the door she sprang from the bed, grabbed the plate and hurled it at his back. It smashed into the wall near his right shoulder and sprayed his jacket with disintegrating vegetables.

CHAPTER FIVE

Brown listened to the exchange on an R/T unit in the lounge. He heard the shattering plate and he sighed. If it wasn't for the money he would have packed up and left Stephen whose personality grated on him. Some might say Stephen's hatred of fringe religions verged on paranoia; others might say that he was a gentle, sympathetic man who was troubled by the frailties of the human condition; and a few might see him simply as a mercenary in an allegorical battle between good and evil, a soldier who could be hired by either side but would always convince himself that he was fighting for good as he pocketed the fee. But whichever way you looked at it, the man was unstable and capable of sudden violent behaviour.

When he walked in, his jacket showing damp stains from where he had sponged it, Brown was pouring a whisky.

'Drinking again,' enquired Stephen.

Brown raised one eyebrow. 'I hope you realise that your threats have set us back at least three days.'

'Do you know what she did?'

'I could guess. She threw food at you. What did you expect after polarising the issue into eating versus bathing? She's no fool. You've got us into a win–lose situation and she'll exploit it.'

'Why do you say that?'

51

'By saying "No deal" you've introduced the element of bargaining. Deals are bargains. Bargains belong to relationships. Relationships are not what we want. In fact, a relationship between her and you or me is the last thing we want.'

'So?'

'All her energies will go into withstanding the temptation to eat unless she's first allowed a bath. It becomes a game. Child versus parent. Deprogramming is not a game.'

'You must have misheard me, Brownie. I didn't make eating any sort of an issue. I said that if she didn't eat then she wouldn't get anything else for twenty-four hours.'

'Don't blame me if she develops *anorexia nervosa*. She's the type, and according to her mother she had a spell of it when she was thirteen.'

Stephen laughed. 'Oh, I see. You think I really am going to wait twenty-four hours before offering more food. I wouldn't dream of it. In that room and without a watch she has no idea of time. She's exhausted now and she'll soon go to sleep. I'll wake her in a couple of hours or so with a bowl of *crudites*, bread and cheese, and tell her she's had a good night's sleep. It's another day. She can take or leave her food but I'll be back in a few minutes as we want to have another little talk.'

Brown downed his drink. 'I accept you're in charge. I accept you've had a few successes in this field. But' – he paused to light a cigarette – 'I know, and you must know, we are not following the established methods of deprogramming.'

Stephen had moved across to the record-player. He was examining the disc on the turntable. 'Can't think why you like this dreary stuff. Let's have something good. Let's have Elvis.'

Brown was not deterred. Replacing the rejected record in its cover, he went on, 'I realise our hands are tied because of the undertaking you gave her parents not to go to extremes, but in my opinion it was a mistake to make such a promise. Successful methods practised in America have established that the subject may be allowed water for drinking, but no food. You have no system. Food is arbitrarily provided.'

'You're providing eggs for your grandmother to suck, Brown.'

'Subjects should not be allowed to sleep during deprogramming. This is the quickest way to wear down resistance. But what do you do? You encourage her to get some sleep. Why don't you provide an electric blanket while you're about it?' The sarcasm in his voice was so biting that each word seemed to leave his mouth equipped with teeth of its own.

'You're wasting your time, Brownie. I know more about this scene than you ever will.'

'And another thing. Her *mantra*. That has to be stopped and the correct way to stop *mantras* is to fill the subject's mouth with ice cubes. But you won't do this. You let her . . .'

His voice was drowned by the opening bars of an Elvis Presley record at full volume.

Raising his voice to a shout he continued, 'And on no account should the subject be allowed to sit. She should stand upright and without any support. But what do you do? You bring in a chair for her. I'm surprised you don't let her have some of the cushions out of this room as well. Make her really comfortable.'

Stephen began clicking his fingers in time with the beat.

'In fact,' Brown shouted, 'the only way you've kept to

53

the book is allowing her no hygiene except going to the loo.'

Stephen turned down the volume. 'I'm surprised you're so keen on the rule-book, Brownie. Thought you were a gambler. Isn't that why you're here? Something to do with a gambling debt and a very hard creditor who's breathing down your neck? Still, if you don't need the cash, and you want to opt out, I'm not stopping you.'

The stolidly-built psychologist whose eyebrows possessed an eloquence of their own allowed them to slump in a vee of dejection. 'Just don't blame me if this is a wash-out,' he muttered.

'I won't.'

Elvis was singing about his baby leaving him and a heart-break hotel. Stephen shuffled jerkily round the room, fingers snapping.

'One other thing,' shouted Brown, 'might I remind you that during deprogramming the subject should be naked. This makes her feel extremely vulnerable and affects self-esteem.'

Stephen stopped his solo dance. 'So that's it. You're a dirty old man, Brown. No better than the dirty old man we're trying to wean her from.'

'Jesus Christ!' Brown grabbed the bottle of whisky and his glass. 'I'll be in my room when you want me,' he said, and stormed out.

She had dark rings under tired eyes but her voice was clear as she gave her *mantra* replies. The *crudites* had been spurned and her persistent refusal to eat was evident in the shadowy hollows of her pale cheeks.

Brown sat close to her, staring at her but saying nothing. He listened with contempt to Stephen's softly probing questions. At times he sounded like an earnest young evangelical attempting to convert a wayward adolescent by friendly persuasion. This was not how deprogramming should operate. The subject should be battered with ridicule, insult and violent abuse at close range, and with the aid of electronic amplification if available. Brown knew that if he were given the chance he would direct a verbal assault aimed at her appearance.

He recalled a moonie who had been brought to him for therapy. She had the same spacey look in her eyes as Caroline but he had changed that when she had been forced to strip and he had seen a strawberry birthmark, the size and shape of a tulip-head, on her navel. He had mocked the flaw and taunted her about it until, ashamed at her nudity and mortified by his thick-fingered attempts to peel off the mark, she had broken down and cried. Within a week she was home with her parents freed from the belief that Sun Myung Moon was the Lord of the Second Advent.

He was thinking about this cure when he heard Stephen say, 'That'll do for now. We'll make this a short session. You just think about what I've said. God is God and greater that the sum of everything. Love is just a small part of this sum. Okay? Now I'll take you back to your room.'

Brown could hardly believe his ears. The session had lasted less than half an hour, most of which had been occupied by Stephen delivering a monologue on false prophets who pleaded special causes, usually their own self-interest, which by definition could be only a fraction of the sum adding up to God. It was incredible to Brown that he should waste time on philosophical and moral questions which were counter-productive to any deprogramming process.

When they were alone together in the lounge, and after

he had poured himself a drink, Brown said, 'This is the last time I'll ever work with you. I can't see us ever collecting the balance of our fee at this rate.'

Stephen picked up a needle and thread. He was sitting with his jacket draped across his lap and was preparing to sew on a button. He licked the thread-end and aimed it at the needle-eye. 'Poor old Brownie,' he said, as soon as the thread was through. 'You'd like a bit of sadistic fun.'

Brown banged his glass down on the table and reached for a cigarette packet. 'Sadistic nothing,' he said indignantly. 'I want to do a proper job. Of itself, deprogramming gives me no kicks at all.'

Stephen began sewing on the button. 'Can't think how you got into this business if it gives you so little pleasure. Technicians fall into two groups. There are the crusaders, like me. And there are the low-mentality thugs with a taste for bullying. But you aren't in either category. Not at first sight. Why do you do it, Brownie?'

They both knew he had been struck off the general medical register for offences involving the sale of drug prescriptions and that he had set himself up as a psychologist, a profession for which no qualifications were necessary and which was not under the control of any supervisory body. He had advertised his services in little magazines which catered for minorities with specific behavioural hang-ups. He offered therapy for those with unwanted homosexual inclinations but the fees he earned had not kept pace with his gambling debts. He had met Stephen at a poorly attended public meeting on the use and abuse of aversion therapy and almost immediately each had seen how the other could be utilized. Stephen needed a new partner – his last partner had been scared by threats of prosecution for forcible abduction and unlawful imprisonment – Brown needed money, and fees for deprogramming were very high.

'Why do you do it, Brownie?'

'Asking that sort of question in that sort of voice indicates an immature personality.'

Stephen looked up so sharply he might have pricked himself on the needle. 'That's not a friendly thing to say.'

The older man, having scored, sat back and nonchalantly tickled ash from his cigarette against the rim of an ashtray. 'We don't have to be friends,' he remarked. 'But we ought to be a team with a common purpose and common means of achieving that purpose.'

Stephen bit off the thread. The button was securely in place. He stood up and put on the jacket.

'Our purpose,' he said, 'is to return Caroline to her loving family purified from her brainwashing by a goat posing as a messiah. It will be a longer than usual process because her family is loving and doesn't want us to use the more extreme methods. I have built up some reputation in this field and it is a reputation for integrity. You have no reputation except as a former drug pedlar and an incompetent card player. That's why what I say goes. And I don't want snide talk of immature personality because I warn you, Brownie, I shan't turn the other cheek.' He went to the record-player. 'Now let's have some musical relief.'

'Not him again for Christ's sake.'

'It's a reissue LP and very good.'

Brown's eyes rolled like wheeling gulls beneath overhanging cliffs. 'How long till we have another verbal,' he asked.

'We'll let her rest and we could do with some sleep. Make it eight hours from now.'

Brown rose to his feet. 'It's useless to tell you that now is *not* the time to relax the pressure.'

'Useless.'

Brown left the room without another word. A blast of rock music followed him.

CHAPTER SIX

Stephen nursed a twelve-bore shot-gun in the crook of his arm as a pale dawn groped its way over the horizon. Acres of flat farmland were still sheathed in darkness but a row of stunted water-willows became silhouetted against the pallid skyline like a train of prehistoric men marching in single file, their shoulders weighed down by carcasses of the hunt.

He was waiting for the wild geese to come flying in from the east. Anyone could pick off the lazy herring gulls that came inland at the first sign of winter but that was sport for the sake of killing, not for the pot. Wild duck were an easier target but few came to this locality, although he knew of a couple of ponds where they sometimes came to rest in the failing light of evening. It was good country for snipe and occasionally he brought one down with a snap shot taken just after it had left the ground and before it was able to wing away on its baffling zigzag flight. But it was the geese he found most challenging. They flew faster and truer than the other birds and with the wind behind them would pass in a swift wedge overhead and be gone.

He wore a dull green rainproof anorak, thick brown denim trousers and heavy rubber boots not only because in this gear it would be difficult for game-birds to see him but also as a protection against the wind which had a chill edge and a saline tang as it swept in from the North Sea, across the desolate salt marshes and over the rich fen farmlands.

He had already waited half an hour and might have to wait another half for the sake of two or three seconds when the birds would be within range. As he kept vigil, scanning the far horizon, he thought of Caroline. She had been with them four days and had changed overnight from a stubborn brainwashed child reciting a magic incantation into a young woman who seemed anxious to please. He hoped the conversion was due to his own patient efforts to communicate, but he wasn't certain; Brown deeply mistrusted the sudden change in her.

She had stopped asking for a bath and seemed to regard the dirt on her dress and body as a just punishment. She was willing to talk about anything and had even condemned the methods used by Irving O and admitted that he had exerted some sort of hypnotic influence over her. Apart from her father, whom she still seemed to dislike intensely, she was happy to talk about her family. Whatever had caused her conversion had happened between going to bed, hollow-eyed and with food untouched, and greeting Stephen next morning with a smile. She had started tucking into breakfast before he had had time to lay it on the table.

'You want my opinion,' Brown had said, 'I think she's shamming. Playing a game. She's decided to be a good girl to get her release. She's no more normalised than when she got here. How can she be when every time she rubs her eyes or pulls a weary face you say, "That's enough. Let's have a rest." '

'There are more ways than one of killing a cat,' Stephen had replied.

Brown gave a snort of derision. 'Kill a cat? Do you think we're treating an ailurophobiac? No wonder we aren't getting anywhere.'

'We have got somewhere,' Stephen had said in a controlled voice. 'We have made a breakthrough by establishing trust, confidence and intellectual *rapport* backed by fairly minimal deprivation.'

Light was spreading across the flat landscape. He could see a barn and other farm outbuildings like specks in the western distance. Soon the agricultural workers would be driving across the fields with the machinery of modern intensive farming at their disposal to exploit each fertile acre to its limit. The beet had been lifted and it was now time to drill winter wheat. He looked back towards the east and licked the salt off his lips. There was still no sign of the geese.

When, in the bitterness of anger and grief at the suicide of his best friend, he had vowed to dedicate himself to fighting the poisonous growth of manipulative religions he had thought of it as a lifetime crusade, but recently the impetus had slowed. What had once been a vocation was becoming a well-paid trade. He needed a new direction for his energies and his thoughts were moving towards a neglected ambition.

The indigenous people of the fens were impoverished and culturally deprived. Illiteracy among children of the poorest families was high and these children, the offspring of generations of inbreeding, had inherited recessive genes and were regarded by outside and uncaring authorities as inferior and retarded. Fenland pride, symbolised long ago by fierce woad-daubed warriors, and then by Queen Boadicea, and then by Hereward the Wake, and then by Oliver Cromwell, and then lastly by ice-skating world

61

champions, was now an all-pervasive apathy. Stephen had a dream of changing this and of being the man to bring pride and a sense of identity back to fen-folk.

He needed only a few more good pay-days from rich parents anxious to reclaim wilful and wayward children from the tentacles of men like Irving O and he would have enough money to begin the fieldwork necessary for an acceptable research project and to fund a pressure group.

His mind was idling on an offshoot of his dream – a medical centre to study rheumatic complaints endemic among fenmen – when the geese swept in from the east in a long low echelon. They passed over the line of stunted willows as, fixing his eyes to an outflanker, his body automatically moved into the ready position. He watched it come in, mounted his gun in one fluent movement, and fired just before the goose arrived vertically overhead. The bird flew on unharmed. He pivoted and fired a second barrel. Not a goose swerved; not a goose fell. He watched them disappear like a thrown javelin over the fields. After emptying the spent cartridges and reloading, he tucked the stock under his armpit and, with muzzles pointing at the ground, he began the walk back to the cottage.

From upstairs came the sound of Brown snoring his way through an alcoholic slumber. A spasm of disgust passed across Stephen's face as he went to Caroline's room to peer through the spy-hole. She was asleep. He knocked and walked in.

She turned and opened sleep-bleared eyes. Shielding them against the bulb in the ceiling which shone day and night she said, 'Hello.'

'Hello. Sleep well?'

'Yes, thanks.'

'I thought you might like fruit juice followed by kippers and hot buttered toast, all washed down with coffee.'

'It sounds super. Plenty of toast and plenty of butter. I could do with putting on a bit of weight.'

'Will do . . . Caroline?'

'Yes?' She wriggled out of the blanket and sat upright on the mattress.

'What made you change your mind about Irving and Eventide Joy?'

'I've told you. I can see it was a racket. It's as simple as that.'

He sat on the end of the bed leaving a space of more than an arm's length between them. 'I don't think it is as simple as that.'

'You mean I'm lying? Putting on a front so that you'll let me go?'

'Maybe. I'm not convinced you're the person you were before you met Irving.'

She smiled. 'How could you be? You didn't know me before I met him.'

'That's not quite what I meant. How do you feel about your immediate family?'

'I told you last night. Have you forgotten?'

'What about your father?'

'I hate him,' she said calmly.

'But why?'

She pulled her knees to her chest and wrapped her arms round them. 'Chemistry. And he's always treated me like a brainless nuisance.'

'He loves you.'

She laughed.

'He does, Caroline.'

'Prove it.'

63

'He's been here to check that you're all right. He looked in on you while you were asleep.'

'I was wondering if they knew where I was.'

'Of course they do.'

'I didn't know he had that much conscience to come up here. There must have been another reason. Perhaps mother nagged at him to look in and as it happened to be on the way to a rich customer or some woman he's taken a fancy to he thought he'd got nothing to lose.'

'I'm sure that just isn't so.'

She turned to look at him. 'I don't know why you should be bothered.'

He met her look with a gaze which spoke mutely of a compulsive sincerity. 'I don't know what nonsense Irving indoctrinated you with, but although Brown and I are technicians we are also human beings and we believe in helping those who need help. We believe in persuasion through understanding, not through fear.'

She gave him a long, cool look. 'That's why you let me wander around that bog half-demented by fright?'

'It was necessary. You were never in danger. The fear was in your mind.'

She unclasped her knees and swung her legs on to the bed so that she could sit facing him. 'Irving told us all about deprogramming and the methods used by people like you. One of the things was transference. He said it was possible in the course of treatment to get sexually attracted to the person who was treating you. Physically I'm not specially attracted by you and I'm most certainly not attracted by Brown – I think he's creepy – but I know equally well that I don't attract you in the least. It's something you give off. . . . Are you afraid of women, Stephen?'

He gave a flinching laugh. 'That'll be the day.'

'Have you a girl friend?'

'Hundreds . . . No, Caroline, we are not going to talk about me. We'll talk about your father.'

'Must we?'

'Why do you dislike him so much?'

'I don't dislike him. I hate him. That's the beginning and end of it.'

'Tell me about him.'

'Oh, God. This is boring. Well, if you must know, he's a very busy businessman. He's got two loves, his work and all the perks that go with it, and sailing. After that, in descending order of priority come his women friends, my brother and a distant cousin living in Australia. Then, a long way behind, comes my mother. I'm not even in the field.'

'He did come up here to see how you were.'

'Great. And the moment he arrived I'll bet he looked at his watch and said, "I think I'll be going now." '

Stephen stood up. 'I'll start your breakfast.'

'Don't forget. Plenty of toast and butter.'

'Is there anything else you want?'

She looked puzzled. 'Such as?'

'You haven't asked for a bath recently.'

'That's right. I haven't. Why should a dirty bitch like me have the luxury of a bath?'

'You are not a dirty bitch. Not any longer.'

She looked grateful for the small tribute and then quickly lowered her eyes like someone who doesn't wish the other person to see that triumph is peeping round the corners of gratitude.

Brown seldom laughed; he had little to laugh about. He

65

was heavily in debt to the boss of a gaming club, his divorced wife was threatening to sue him for alimony arrears, the tax inspector was on his trail for undeclared earnings, his doctor had told him to stop smoking on account of a heart condition and he suffered from depression for which he was being treated by a tricyclic drug. This drug produced side effects of mouth dryness and periodic sweating which was another reason why he seldom laughed. But when Stephen suggested that the dramatic change in Caroline's mental health was due to spontaneous remission he had to laugh. It was a mirthless sound. 'Spontaneous remission! That's a good one,' he said, and laughed again.

They were eating breakfast in the kitchen.

Stephen wished he had never gone into partnership with the nonentity who had a faceless face and caterpillar eyebrows. The man was getting on his nerves. When they first met he had been impressed by Brown's knowledge of the latest behaviourist theories and that he seemed unafraid of the risk of being prosecuted for holding people against their will. Stephen was also curious about his claims to be able to give therapeutic help to those burdened with unwanted inclinations towards homosexuality.

Stephen was unable to face his own sexual problem. Whenever realisation of its true nature became too close for comfort he would sheer away from thinking about it. He had never asked Brown about the therapy used for treating homosexuals, and Brown had never offered any information, and yet it was the claim to success in this field which had clinched the partnership deal. But now, facing Brown over the debris of a meal, he decided that the sooner the partnership was dissolved the better.

66

'What is so funny about my saying the change in Caroline's mental attitudes is due to spontaneous remission,' he asked coldly.

Brown wiped his mouth clean of crumbs and mirth. 'Of course it happens,' he said. 'Neurotic disorders can clear up without any treatment. Denker's famous study proves it. And other studies have shown that most neurotic disorders are self-terminating after about two or three years.' He spoke seriously as he didn't like the look in Stephen's eyes. 'But the phenomenon of spontaneous remission is little understood. I doubt if it would occur in a case like Caroline's. And anyway, she's been receiving treatment from us, not the right treatment in my opinion, but she's had treatment and so remission can hardly be spontaneous in the sense commonly used.'

Stephen poured himself another cup of tea. 'You think she's faking recovery so that we'll let her go free?'

'I think so.'

'How could we check?'

Brown thought deeply. The professional side of his personality hadn't been so warped that he didn't want to achieve a genuine cure, but cupidity and the need for quick cash tempted him to take his share of the fee and disappear. He struck a compromise. 'Let me have her alone for a couple of hours. No interruptions. And I'll find out whether she's trying to fool us.'

Stephen seemed to weigh the suggestion. 'All right,' he said at length. 'You're on.'

'No interruptions.'

'Fair enough. There's a down-pipe outside which needs repairing. I'll work on that.'

'Care for a side bet,' asked Brown.

'On what?'

'That I'll be able to show she's faked recovery, or spontaneous remission, or whatever you like to call it.'

'I don't gamble with money.'

'Only with people,' said Brown caustically, rising from his chair and leaving the table.

CHAPTER SEVEN

Stephen picked up the tray. She had eaten everything, even the kipper skins.

'You've improved greatly, Caroline. I wish I could be sure it was a permanent improvement.'

'I never want to see or hear of Irving again. That man is evil.'

'He is. But what made you see the light?'

'I just did. It's as simple as that. Maybe it was something you said when you were talking to me. I don't know. There are some things you can't explain. How do you explain falling out of love?'

Stephen stood holding the tray like a man uncertain whether to go or stay. 'I'm willing to be convinced,' he said, 'but Brown isn't.'

She pulled a face. 'I can't help that.'

'Maybe you can.'

'How?'

'Brown would like to see you alone.'

'No, thanks.'

'You don't really have any option, Caroline.'

She ran her fingers through the long auburn hair as though combing it and then looked ruefully at her dirty fingernails. 'What do I have to say or do to prove I've finished with Irving,' she asked.

'Just tell the truth.'

'But I've told the truth.'

'Tell it to Brown.'

A note of fear crept into her voice. 'He won't hurt me? I'm not very good at standing physical pain.'

'Nothing like that. If you tell the truth you've nothing to worry about . . . Come along.'

She stood up reluctantly and smoothed the creases in her shabby dress. 'All right. Let's get it over with,' she said.

Brown was already waiting in the deprogramming room smoking a large cigar. She went to her usual chair and sat down. Stephen left, and Brown turned the key in the door. 'I did that,' he said, pocketing the key, 'not to keep you in but to keep anyone else out. From now on it's just you and me, girl. Understand?'

She nodded.

'Answer when I speak to you!'

'Yes,' she said.

He sat down in front of her so that their knees were almost touching. After staring at her fixedly for a few moments he blew a plume of smoke in her face. Her eyelids shuttered with stinging distaste and her body recoiled slightly.

'You don't like me, do you, girl?'

'I don't know you.'

'Don't give me that. You know me. Stop playing games. Now give me a straight answer. You don't like me, do you?'

'I like you all right.'

'Liar. You're a liar, girl. A dirty deceitful liar. What are you?'

She lowered her head submissively. 'I'm a liar,' she whispered.

'That's another lie, isn't it? Pretending to admit you're a liar is just another lie, isn't it?'

'How do you mean?'

'Call me Mr Brown when you speak to me.'

'How do you mean, Mr Brown?'

'I mean that inside yourself you don't think you're a liar, but you say "I'm a liar" in the hope that I'll go easy with you. But I won't. Now give me the real answer. Are you or are you not a dirty deceitful liar?'

'I am a liar.'

'And you've lied about your change of heart, haven't you?'

'No, Mr Brown.'

'What caused the sudden conversion, girl?'

'I don't know, Mr Brown. Honestly I don't know.'

'Honestly? That's a laugh.' He gave a laugh. 'Listen to the liar being honest.'

She kept her head bowed and her body seemed tense with the effort of trying to contract into itself, to make herself as small as possible.

'Look at me,' he shouted.

She lifted her head.

'God, you're filthy,' he said. 'There's dirt on your face and you stink. I thought this cigar might cover your smell but it doesn't.' He blew some more smoke at her. 'That's for fumigation. Why do you smell so filthy, girl?'

'I haven't washed, Mr Brown.'

'It's not normal healthy dirt you smell of, the dirt of an honest worker. Yours is a putrid and corrupt smell; a foul bad meat, bad fish smell. Does Irving smell bad like that too?'

She trembled slightly.

71

'Answer me, girl! Does Irving smell like you? Do you smell of him?'

'I don't know, Mr Brown.'

'Lying again. You're a lying whore. What are you?'

The tremor of her body inflected her voice. 'A lying whore, Mr Brown.'

'Let's see your hands. Hold them out.'

She presented her hands.

'Filthy.'

She lowered her hands as though ashamed.

'Now stand on the chair.'

'Stand?'

'I said stand. Stand. Stand. Stand. I want to look at your feet.'

Shakily she stepped on to the chair's seat.

'Get back where you were,' he said. 'I can't stand the sight. I find dirty, smelly feet utterly repulsive. In fact, I find you repulsive, but I've got a job to do.' He flicked cigar ash on her dress. 'You'd be a gift to a Freudian analyst, girl. Did you know that?'

'No.'

'Why do you think I say that?'

'I don't know, Mr Brown.'

'So you're unintelligent as well as being a dirty whore?'

She lowered her head.

'Look at me when I'm speaking to you, girl!'

She raised her head. Her eyes were moist.

'I'll spell it out to you. You couldn't commit incest with your father so Irving was the father substitute. Am I right?'

She turned her head away. He reached out and placed his hand on her cheek, turning her to face him again.

'When you go back to Irving remember what I've said.'

'I'm not going back to him.'

'Lying again. I've never met such a liar.'

'I'm not. Please believe me.'

'Please believe me,' he mimicked. 'Why should I believe you, girl? Give me one reason why I should believe you.'

She was silent.

'What's the matter? Haven't you got a lie ready?'

Tears had come to her eyes and she was trembling more violently.

'You want to get out of here,' he continued, 'and you think that if you say some hard things about Irving we'll let you go. But we know it's a sham. The moment you leave you'd go looking for Irving or his likeness. You're a sick girl. What do you say to that?'

'What can I say,' she asked desperately.

'You can tell the truth. The naked truth. Maybe if you were stripped you'd be more truthful. Clothes conceal. Nudity and truth go together.' He fingered her dress. 'What sort of a corpse would we find under this filthy shroud?'

'No,' she breathed.

'Take it off.'

'No.'

'You'll do as you're told, girl. Strip!'

'I won't.'

'Up!'

She blinked and her body jerked.

'Up! Up! Up! Get up when I tell you!'

'Up!' As he spoke he stood, grabbed her by the scruff of her dress and hauled her to her feet. A kick sent her chair skidding across the room.

'Stand there.' He positioned her about two feet from the wall and then sat down to regard her. 'You look as if you've been dug up. You're not a girl or a woman, you're an it. A corpse. Take off your burial shroud, you corpse!'

73

She shook her head.

'Right. I'll do it for you.'

As he rose to his feet there was a banging on the door and Stephen's voice shouted, 'Open!'

'Go away.'

'Open or I'll blast it open.'

Brown threw his cigar on the floor and stamped on it. 'Why do you have to interfere just as I was getting somewhere,' he asked as he opened the door.

The next moment both men were on the floor, clawing and punching.

Stephen ended on top, gripping Brown's neck-tie and pulling at the knot. Brown crooked the fingers of both hands into his collar to prevent himself being strangled. Both men were breathing heavily. Stephen relaxed slightly and Brown took advantage of the off-guard moment to grab Stephen's hair, twist it, and heave himself clear. Both men scrambled to their feet. They looked at each other like animals of different species who were natural enemies in the wild.

'Get out,' said Stephen.

'Not until you've paid me my share.'

'You won't get anything from me. I promised there wouldn't be any extreme stuff. You broke that promise.'

'Your promise, not mine. I want my share.'

'Get lost.'

Brown made an incoherent sound and began to charge forward like an enraged bull but he stumbled and fell.

'Get up and get out,' said Stephen.

Brown lay motionless.

Caroline spoke. 'I think he's passed out,' she said in a faint voice.

Stephen crouched down. After a few moments he looked

up. 'I think he's had it.' He stood up looking pale and shocked.

'Are you sure?'

'He's not breathing. There's no pulse beat.'

'What are you going to do?' Her voice was firmer and of the two she seemed less disturbed and more in control.

'I ought to call a doctor.'

'A doctor can't do anything except give a death certificate. And what would he give as the cause of death?'

'Heart failure,' replied Stephen. 'It must have been heart failure. You saw it all. He came at me and then fell. I didn't touch him.'

'You didn't touch him then but you nearly strangled him a few seconds before. I'll bet his neck is marked. How will you explain that?'

He looked at her rather vacantly. 'I don't know.'

She moved across to where Brown's body lay. 'What a fool,' she said contemptuously. 'Incest!' She gave a sour laugh. 'He couldn't have been more wrong.'

'I ought to get an ambulance. Notify the police.'

'Why don't you then?'

He didn't reply.

'I'll tell you why,' she continued. 'If you call the police you'd have to explain this set-up and explain how Brown came to die with marks on his neck. You'd have to explain how you took me by force and kept me a prisoner here against my will.'

An expression of anguish creased his fresh, schoolboyish face and he looked the man he might be ten years hence when the last lustre of youth had faded. 'God, what a mess!' he said.

'Your mess,' she replied coolly.

75

'I know. But look, Caroline, I need your help. Your co-operation.'

'Why should I co-operate?' She sounded and looked like someone who is indifferent to whatever answer might be given.

'I treated you all right,' he said. 'I was intending to let you go.'

'You wouldn't let me have a bath.'

'Yes, I'm sorry about that.'

'But I'll have a bath now.'

'Yes, of course. But what are we going to do about Brown?'

A sort of amused triumph came to her face. 'Are you asking for suggestions?'

'Have you got any?'

She shrugged. 'Lose him.'

'Lose him? How?'

'This is the back of beyond, isn't it? Does anyone ever come here?'

'Not often.' He thought. 'I could lose him in the marsh. I know a place. A bit of pressure from above and he'd be lost forever.'

'That's your answer then.'

They looked at each other.

'Do it,' she said in a softer voice.

'What about you?'

'I shan't run away.'

'You . . .'

'I'll stay.'

'I'd better wait until night. I might be seen.'

She nodded. 'Leave him here.'

'No. I'll take him outside. To the shed.'

'Can you manage on your own?'

'I can drag him. I'll use the van to take him to the edge of the marsh.'

'Fine. Now I'm going to have that bath. And' – she looked at her fingernails – 'I'm going to cut these. Can I have some scissors?'

'Yes. What about your dress?'

She looked with distaste at the muddy shift. 'Have you got anything I could wear? We're about the same size. Any old slacks and a sweater would do.'

'I can manage that.'

'And don't forget the scissors. My nails are shocking.'

A couple of minutes later, after he had put a pair of faded brown slacks and a loose-knit green sweater on top of an Ali Baba basket in the bathroom, he called out, 'Hey, Caroline, I haven't got any shoes for you.'

She joined him. 'Don't worry. I'm used to going around barefoot. Now you run along and leave me.'

'You're not thinking of climbing out of the window?'

'No, I'm not thinking of climbing out of the window. Now you get on with what's got to be done.'

She gently pushed him out of the bathroom and he heard the lock shut fast.

As he returned to the deprogramming room he decided that once he had got Brown's body inside the van he would weight it with bricks. It might make a more difficult haul over the marsh but it would make the interment as untraceable as a burial at sea.

CHAPTER EIGHT

The job took longer than he expected and by the time he returned to the cottage she had had her bath and was waiting for him in the lounge.

'Look at these slacks,' she giggled. 'They make me look like an old movie comic.'

He gaped at her. 'What have you done with your hair,' he exclaimed.

The auburn tresses had gone. Her head was covered with a close-cropped reddish fuzz.

'I cut it off.'

'But why?'

'I've had an idea.' She flopped into the armchair which Brown usually occupied and gazed around. 'Did you furnish this yourself?'

'What idea?' He looked bewildered.

'In a minute. You're impatient.' She continued gazing around. 'Not much taste,' she pronounced. 'Nothing really goes, does it? Patterned curtains and patterned carpet, and each shouts at the other.'

He sat on the arm of another chair. 'Why did you cut your hair?'

She smiled and caressed the top of her head with finger-tips. 'Do you like it? My new style.'

'It's all right.'

'It doesn't make me look too masculine?'

'Er, no.'

'One thing in favour of this sweater. You can't see how flat-chested I am.'

He shifted uneasily on the chair-arm. 'You cut your hair,' he said, 'because you want to make a new start. By changing your appearance you are symbolically making a fresh start.'

'That's right. You're clever. But talking of fresh things. that bath-water wasn't very fresh. There were some horrible tiny wriggling things in the water.'

'Well, yes, I should have told you. It's a peculiar water system here. There's a well in front and a bucket to draw water but the bucket is hardly ever used these days. Some pipes run from the well to the cottage and an electric pump brings up the water. The tanks for the bathroom aren't purified but a separate tank which supplies the kitchen has a special filter and the water is absolutely pure.'

'What were the wriggling things,' she asked.

'Insect larvae.'

She shuddered. 'Ugh! Anyway, I feel clean. A new woman . . . Did you choose those curtains? They're awful.'

'Do we have to talk about curtains?'

'I'm curious. Is this your taste?'

He sighed. 'All right. I'll play along. I used to own this place but I sold it to someone influential in the political world. He knows what my business is, and he approves. I reclaimed his son from the Scientologists. He uses it as a holiday retreat. Loves the district. He's an authority on marsh grasses and flowers. I can have it for a fairly nominal rent whenever he isn't using it. Oh, yes. The furnishings. It's his taste.'

She studied her newly manicured nails and he noticed

that her fingers were short and her palms broad. They were practical hands; the sort he preferred. For a few moments neither spoke. She seemed completely at ease lounging casually in the armchair, right leg inelegantly crooked so that its ankle rested on top of her left knee. She was so unlike the girl who had arrived at the cottage she might have been another person.

'Shall I call your parents or will you,' he asked.

'What were the terms? How much were you given for grabbing me off the street and bringing me here? What's the going charge for a deprogramming session?'

'Two thousand. One thousand down and one thousand at the end when the subject has been returned to normal. If there's no cure – and that hasn't happened yet – then the initial thousand is returned less expenses.'

She blew between her teeth. 'Phew. It isn't cheap.' And then, as though she didn't believe it, 'You're not going to tell me my father paid over a thousand. Not for me.'

'Yes, I am. I've told you, Caroline, your parents care about you.'

'Then why didn't they show it? Why was my father always against me and my mother always backing him up?' He searched for a reply but before he could find one she continued, 'And so you're still owed a thousand?'

'That's right.'

'You took a risk. What if Irving had notified the police?'

'People like Irving never do. They've got too much to hide.'

She nodded agreement. 'I'll phone my mother and tell her I'm well and happy and feel a new woman, and I'll be on my way home fairly soon.'

He frowned. 'Fairly soon?'

'Let's not rush this. I'd like to spend a bit more time

here. With you. Don't worry I'm not getting a yen for you. It's just that I enjoyed our conversations. They weren't a bit like Irving said we should expect. But if it's not mutual I'll leave now.'

He went across to the window. It was a dull morning with a lowering, overcast sky. The wind, still blowing strongly, ruffled the top of a thorn hedge, and a pair of young ash trees swayed and bent like two dancers responding to a melody in the wind.

He spoke with his back to her. 'I'd like you to stay a while,' he said. 'I've enjoyed talking with you.'

'Fine.'

He turned. 'What was this idea you talked about earlier? You said something about an idea.'

'Forget it . . . Incidentally, you'll be lucky if you see that thousand.'

'What do you mean?'

'You don't know my father. He'll laugh in your face and tell you to sue.'

'He didn't seem that sort of man.'

'If he seemed nice it was eyewash. That man can be charming to anyone but the moment their use to him is finished . . .' She made a chopping gesture with her hand.

'Why do you dislike him so much?'

She shifted her position so as to cross her legs. Although she was wearing slacks her hands went instinctively to pull down a skirt. 'It's not easy to explain,' she said, 'except by examples. For instance, when I was a kid I used to take a cat with me to bed at night for company. Mother knew about it, but he didn't. When he found out he was very angry and forbade me to do it any more. He said the cat had fleas and was unhygienic. Well, I didn't take up the cat for four nights but on the fifth I smuggled it up. My father

82

found out and killed it. He said that by my behaviour I had sentenced it to death. Its death was my responsibility.'

'I see. That doesn't make him sound so good.'

'And there was another instance. Do you want to hear about it?'

'Go on.'

'I think I've mentioned he's got a boat. It's his big relaxation. Whenever he had a free week-end and the weather was fair we used to have a compulsory day afloat. I hated it. I've always been afraid of the sea. I used to huddle in the cabin. One day my brother was ill and Mother stayed behind with him. It was just my father and me. When we were right out at sea he dragged me from the cabin and said he was going to teach me to overcome my fears. He forced a life-jacket on me and tried to push me overboard. He said he was teaching me to have confidence and it was for my own good. I fought like mad and in the end he gave up but only on condition that I wouldn't say anything to Mother when we got back. I promised. I would have promised anything.'

Stephen gave her a doubting look.

'Don't you believe me.' she asked.

'Well, yes. Why not?'

'He can charm the birds off a tree when he wants to. That's what's taken him to the top of his business. Charm and ruthlessness. At home my brother got the charm. I got the ruthlessness, and Mother mostly got indifference . . . Do you know how old his latest mistress is?'

Stephen shook his head.

'Eighteen. One year younger than me.' She gazed down at the slacks. 'These look dreadful. I'll go and wash my dress. I can iron it dry. Have you got an iron?'

'In a cupboard in the kitchen.'

She stood up and held the waistband in her hands. 'Mind if I go and do some washing then?'

'I'll join you.'

'You're welcome, but I warn you these slacks are coming off when I get into the kitchen.'

'Oh.'

'Maybe you've got some work to do on the van.'

'Not really.'

'Oh, yes. It's a bit grisly. I forgot. Funny how easy it is to forget someone like him.'

'I'll take the boards off the window of your room. I promised the owner I'd leave the place as I found it.'

'I just need a funny hat and an umbrella and I'd be Charlie Chaplin,' she said, strutting flat-footed.

'What about ringing your mother,' he called after her.

'I'll do it later.'

As the boards came off and daylight seeped into the room which was nothing more than a storage extension at one end of the cottage Stephen thought about his employers. Mrs Moore didn't seem to be the inadequate portrayed by Caroline. It was she who had given him a cheque for a thousand pounds after asking many searching questions and examining written recommendations from others whom Stephen had helped. Her husband hadn't been present at the first meeting, he had only appeared on the scene after Caroline had been taken.

Good-looking in a florid way he seemed the sort of man who knew exactly how to pace himself. He would never burn too much energy at the beginning of a race but would put everything into a killing finish. And yet, even when idling, he could project the qualities of drive, ambition and the will to win. On his visit to the cottage he had listened to Stephen's progress report not so much with patience as with severely curbed impatience. He had made a remark about parental responsibility as though this were a burden to be carried with a rueful smile. On the other hand he had said all the right things about wanting Caroline restored to normal mental health even if (as Caroline had guessed) he had glanced at his watch while he was speaking.

How would he react to her changed appearance?

With cropped hair and loose sweater she almost looked like a boy. Most women made him feel threatened, others brought out a sense of deep respect because in some way they reminded him of his mother, but for Caroline he felt the stirrings of the emotional warmth which had been missing since his friend's suicide.

How did she feel about him?

They had a common bond in the weighted body in the back of the van. He was glad he hadn't telephoned for a doctor or an ambulance. It was better to bury the unloved and unmourned Brown who, so far as his creditors were concerned, was already missing.

He stacked the boards in a corner and opened the window to allow fresh air to dissipate the faint smell of marsh mud and stale cigar smoke. As he moved away he noticed the unfinished cigar Brown had stamped on. Picking it up as though it were an infected article he went to the kitchen to put it in the waste disposal unit.

'Can I come in.' he called.

'Sure.'

She was standing bent over an ironing board, her back to the door. She was naked from the waist down. The brown slacks lay in a heap in one corner.

He dropped the cigar butt in the unit.

'Hello,' she said, without turning.

He could see steam rising as the iron was pressed on the damp dress. Her bare legs were slim and she had small buttocks.

'Sorry,' he said. 'I'd forgotten . . . I'll go and . . .'

'You don't have to go,' she interrupted, still without looking at him. 'You can stay and talk. What does my hair look like from that angle?'

'It looks all right.'

'Do you really think so?'

'Yes.'

'Do you like it better this way or like it was before?'

'I think I like it better as it is.'

As she moved the iron, her hips swayed. He found himself becoming mesmerised and deliberately looked away. He stared at the electric cooker. And then he looked back at her swaying buttocks.

'This is taking ages,' she said. 'I'm quite worn out. Do you want a go?'

As she spoke, she turned. He wrenched his eyes away.

'What's the matter, Stephen?'

His face was burning and his mouth was dry. 'Nothing.'

She switched off the iron, came across and took his hand. 'This horrid business has been a strain, hasn't it?'

'I'm all right.'

'You look as though you could do with a rest. It must have been awful getting him into the back of the van.'

'I'm all right. Really.'

'I think you could do with a rest. It won't be easy doing what you've got to do tonight. Come along.'

She led him out of the kitchen.

'No,' he said, but he followed.

She led him upstairs.

86

'Not in there,' he managed to say. 'That was where Brown slept.'

'Which is your room?'

'That one.'

She entered, released his hand and went to draw the curtains. He stood uncertainly at the door.

'I like these more than the ones downstairs,' she said. 'They're a pretty shade of green.'

He seemed to have lost the power of speech and movement.

'Don't stand there,' she said, pulling back the bed covers. 'Take off your shoes and get in.'

Like someone who is fearful and yet resigned to his fate he obeyed her order.

When he was lying down she climbed in beside him.

'That's better,' she said. 'We're two of a kind, you and me. Lost lady, lost man.'

CHAPTER NINE

Her head was cradled in his arm as they lay on their backs. 'You don't mind talking about it then,' she asked.

'There's nothing much to talk about. Not now.' He turned his neck to kiss her forehead lightly.

'I sensed it quite early on,' she said. 'When everyone else is coming out and telling whoever'll listen whether they prefer their own or the opposite sex you go to the other extreme. You swim against the stream.'

'I can't explain it.'

'Paradox. Someone once said that paradoxes are the only truth.'

They were still on their backs but not touching except for clasped hands.

'Shall I tell you my idea,' she asked.

'Yes. Go on.'

'It's a game really. But suppose I didn't go home, and suppose my parents thought I'd been kidnapped and they had to pay a ransom. Suppose my father had to pay a hundred thousand, or even fifty thousand. If he paid up I'd really believe he did care.'

He lay on his side watching her dress.

'But where,' he asked, 'where could I be holding you?'

'Not you as you. You as Brown.'

'All right. Where could I, pretending to be Brown, hold you? Obviously it couldn't be here. And my London pad would be no use.'

'My father's boat. It's perfect. He doesn't use it from October on. It's laid up for the winter. It's moored in a creek off the River Colne, less than a hundred miles from here. If we were found it would show that it wasn't a serious kidnapping. What kidnapper would hold his victim in the boat of the man he was trying to extort money from?'

She drew back the curtains. He was putting on his shoes.

'It's an offence to waste police time,' he said, 'and he'd be sure to call in the police.'

'Not necessarily, particularly if he's told that I'll be killed if the police are informed.'

'But if this is all down to Brown, what about me? Your father, or the police, will be looking for me.'

'You can go and see him. Leave me in the boat. You can say that Brown knocked you out and tied you up, and disappeared with me. You've no idea where we are but you'd do anything to help.'

Stephen shook his head. 'I can't see your father saying, "That's fine. Do come in." He's more likely to take a swipe at me. And what about my thousand?'

'I've already told you. He'll let you whistle for it. Tell you to sue him. That thousand has already gone down the drain.'

'I don't like it, Caroline. It's impractical. You're not really serious, are you?'

'It's practical and I'm deadly serious.'

They were in the kitchen and he had just folded up the ironing board.

'Suppose he takes no notice of the ransom demand.'

'Then I shall know what he thinks of me.'

'But you say you know what he thinks about you. According to you, he can't stick you.'

'And according to you, he cares. So who is right?'

Stephen plugged in the kettle to make a pot of tea. For a few moments he didn't speak. Then he asked, 'What would we do if he paid the money over? We couldn't keep it.'

'Naturally we couldn't. You could hand it back less the one thousand he owes you.'

'No. It's a crazy plan. It wouldn't work.'

'Okay. Good-bye.' She moved towards the door.

He jumped in her way. 'Where are you going?'

'Away.'

'Where?'

'I don't know. Maybe back to Irving. Get out of my way, please.'

'You can't mean it.'

'You think I'm crazy.'

'I said the *plan* was crazy.'

'You're not willing to try it for my sake.'

'I didn't say that. Let me think a bit more.'

In the background Elvis was singing softly that he couldn't help falling in love.

'All you need is some capital,' she said. 'Then you could concentrate on your study of the fen people. I think it's a terrific idea. Interesting too. I never knew the eel-fishers were driven out by land-grabbing investors and their traditional fishing territory stolen from them.'

'As you say, I need capital. I don't want this to be just another grant-aided thesis. I want action. I want to see this area revitalised and with its own positive identity. At present it's just a factory. One big farming factory.'

'A hundred thousand would go a long way.'

A troubled look came to his eyes. 'You're not suggesting that if I get the money I should keep it?'

Her eyes remained untroubled. 'Of course not. I'm dreaming aloud.'

They sat down to a meal.

'Is this boat provisioned,' he asked.

'No. We take our own, although there's stuff like sugar and dried milk on board.'

'But we shall be seen. People who know you will see you. They could tell your father.'

'Why should they? They won't know I've been kidnapped. Part of the demand will be that neither the police nor the Press are informed.'

'That sort of request won't stop a man like your father.'

She rose from the table and fetched something wrapped in newspaper. 'No, but this will.'

'What is it?'

'Open it.'

He put down a fork and unfolded the paper. A mass of auburn hair was exposed.

'You send some of that with the ransom demand,' she said, 'and he'll know Brown isn't kidding. The note can say, "Next time it will be a finger".'

He pushed his plate away.

'What's the matter,' she asked.

'I'm not really hungry.'

92

'I am,' she said pronging her fork into spaghetti bolognaise.

'Caroline, when you cut off your hair had you already thought of this plan?'

She looked up. 'I can't honestly say. I cut it for a mixture of reasons. A new start for one. You were right there. Also, I wanted to make myself more attractive to you. I thought you might like me better with short hair. And I may have thought of my father. It's a chicken-and-egg situation. I don't know which came first but I do know that you were the most important.'

The wind had dropped and the sky cleared to a hazy blue. It was an unexpectedly mild afternoon. She was sitting in the back porch writing while he stood a few paces away repairing a down-pipe which led into a galvanised iron water-butt. 'Listen to this,' she said.

'I am writing this at the dictation of Mr X. He has just cut off all my hair some of which is enclosed. He says this is a warning to you not to tell the police or the Press that I am missing. If you don't do exactly as he says, *including not telling anyone that I have been abducted for real,* he says he will cut off my fingers one by one and send them to you and Mother. That's all for now. A demand will follow so start getting your assets cashed.

Caroline.'

'You must hate him,' he said, 'but you're doing this to your mother and brother too.'

She gave a cold almost sightless look which reminded him of how she had been at the beginning. 'You can't make an omelet without breaking eggs.'

93

'Okay.'

'She never stood up for me.'

'Okay. Do we mail it on our way to this place where the boat is moored?'

'No. You take it and mail it as soon as I've done it up in a parcel. Send it by express post. It must arrive at home tomorrow morning.'

He left the down-pipe and came across to her. 'It'll come as a hell of a shock to them.'

'I hope so. Parents who arrange for their children to be brainwashed by deprogrammers deserve to be shocked.'

'I didn't brainwash you. I just helped you to straighten yourself out.'

She smiled up at him. 'I wasn't thinking of you. I was thinking of Brown. That reminds me, we've still got to put this down to Brown. I'll do that while you go to the post office. I suppose they have post offices in this dump.'

It was a slur on the area which previously she had said she found interesting. He appeared not to notice it. 'What are you going to do?'

'I shall call Mother on the phone. I'll say I'm coming home and completely cured of Irving. I'll tell her that you've been marvellous but I can't bear Brown. I shall build you up as the honest, decent guy, and I shall say I don't trust Brown an inch. I'll say he's got a sadistic streak and would have liked to have got me alone and I can't think what my father was doing hiring someone like him. That'll sound familiar. The knock at my father . . . Then I'll sign off with a bright "Be seeing you." '

He reached out very tentatively and stroked the top of her head. She smiled, took his hand and kissed it.

The village was an agglomeration of square, slate-roofed,

red-brick buildings which squatted before a flintstone church like bored pupils round a dull teacher. The only reward for truancy was a visit to the mission hall, or one of the two pubs, or to the village store which doubled as a sub post office. An air of sleepy indifference and apathy seemed to pervade the main street and the inhabitants seemed to consist of women wearing clothes which looked handed down from a previous generation, a few undersized children and old men with faces seamed by grim winters and hard summers. It was almost exactly like a dozen other villages in the catchment area but it was one where Stephen wasn't known. A post-mistress with thin white hair and weatherbeaten face took his packet without comment and issued a receipt while carrying on a conversation with another woman about the price of onions.

He climbed into the van and began the drive back to the cottage. For a few moments he felt shadowy fears about Caroline's plan. He, the authority on manipulative techniques, had the uneasy feeling that he was being manipulated. In some ways she was emotionally unstable, even neurotic, but she could also be coolly cunning and self-possessed. And yet she had done something for him out of what could only be love and he felt a deep sense of gratitude. She had helped him overcome his own damaging neurosis which had poisoned relationships with younger women since a humiliating night with a prostitute in Cambridge.

His apprehensions became submerged in a renewed surge of gratitude. As he drove up the straight and narrow road which ran like an elevated causeway between an endless sea of fields he began to feel cheerful and started to hum one of his favourite Elvis songs.

By arrangement with the cottage owner he was responsible for leaving the place clean and tidy. He would have to go round checking that there were no traces of Brown. The man's belongings, including his operatic records, could be buried with him. Apart from this, only the bed linen had to be removed as this wasn't supplied by the owner.

He and Caroline would wait until dusk, bury the body, and set off for the creek near the mouth of the River Colne. Caroline had said there was a dinghy near a disused warehouse which they could use to get them to the yacht. The van could be parked behind the warehouse and could be moved to different places from time to time to avoid arousing suspicions that it had been abandoned.

He pulled up near the well, a few yards from the cottage's front porch, and switched off the engine. A faint sound from the rear made a prickle run up his spine to the nape of his neck. It was as if a mouse with tiny electric paws had scampered up his back. He heard the sound again and mice feet pattered over his scalp.

After stumbling in his haste to get out of the driving seat he raced to the back of the van and unlocked the door.

A moan came from the shrouded bundle that was Brown.

He climbed inside and began unfastening the length of rope which he had wound round some old blankets. The knots were secure and seemed to take an eternity to undo but eventually he wrenched the top blanket free.

Brown's sparse hair was ruffled and his eyebrows looked like two balls of fur which had been thrown at his forehead and stuck at random.

'I thought you were dead!' Stephen frantically loosened the rope.

Brown's lips moved. 'I don't feel so good.'

'I'll get you to a hospital.'

Bricks clanked against the van's metal floor as Stephen finally pulled the blankets clear.

'Can't lift my arm,' said Brown. 'Paralysed, I think.'

'Don't worry. I'll get help. I just don't understand. I could have sworn you'd had it. No heart-beat.'

The ghost of a smile hovered over Brown's mouth. 'Must have been spontaneous remission,' he whispered.

Stephen burst into the cottage and ran to the phone. Caroline came out of the lounge.

'What are you doing?'

'Trying to get an ambulance. Brown's alive. We made a mistake.'

He banged on the receiver. 'What's the matter with this damn thing?'

'I've cut the line.'

'You've what!'

'After I rang Mother I cut the line. We don't want any calls back. My father might take it into his mind to make a check. Better that the line is out of order.'

Stephen replaced the useless receiver. 'I've got to get him to a hospital myself then.'

'Why?'

'For treatment, of course. The intensive care unit.'

She moved across to him and rested her hand on his arm. 'Don't spoil it.'

'Spoil it?'

She lowered her head so that he couldn't see the expression on her face.

'He shouldn't be moved,' she said quietly. 'The drive could finish him off. You can make some sort of stretcher and we'll get him indoors. Then you can go for an ambulance.'

97

She looked up quickly, trying to read his reaction.

He looked confused.

'I'll get a cushion for his head,' she went on, her voice more firm and confident. 'And I'll stay with him to comfort him while you knock together a stretcher.'

'If you think . . . ?'

'I'm certain it would be fatal for him to have another bumpy ride in that van. I know what it's like in the back. Remember?'

She climbed inside the van holding two cushions. 'You don't deserve this,' she said, 'after the way you treated me. You deserve to suffer like I did.'

His lips moved soundlessly.

'You told me I smelled. You stink. I can't stand the stink. Let's see if these cushions will stop it.'

Stephen was hammering furiously at the frame of a make-shift stretcher. He looked up as she came towards him.

'You needn't bother,' she said. 'He's dead.'

'Are you sure?'

'Positive. I was just getting inside when I heard the death rattle. He really has died this time. Go and see for yourself.'

As he hurried off she returned to the lounge and carefully replaced the cushions, patting them as if to remove any trace of the imprint of a face.

Stephen was determined not to make the same mistake twice but after crouching by the body for some minutes he was convinced that Brown was dead.

He climbed out of the van and stretched his cramped limbs. He knew he was on the brink of one of those moments when a decision made one way or the other could irrevocably alter the direction of his life. Up to this point he had allowed himself to be persuaded by Caroline without considering his own position. But now he saw the real alternatives. The choice was simple enough. He could either wash his hands of her, report to the police what had happened and take the chance of being prosecuted, or he could go along with her plans.

Reason favoured the former, but reason had nothing to do with the sense of gratitude and love he felt. Reason could argue that he was totally infatuated by her, but the emotional answer to this was 'so what?' For the first time as an adult he felt a sexually complete man and the pleasure and satisfaction this gave overwhelmed any rational argument. If this was blind infatuation, so be it.

He went back into the cottage. Caroline threw her arms round his neck. 'Don't ever leave me, Stephen.'

He held her close. 'I won't.'

As they embraced he closed his eyes. Hers remained wide open and she scanned the titles of a row of books in front of her. Most of them were historical or geographical and concerned with localities in East Anglia. A boring collection, she thought.

CHAPTER TEN

Colonel Camber sat squarely in the chair opposite Samson, cleared his throat as though about to bark a command, and said, 'First, any results?'

'No. My only lead is that one of the men may have a cottage near a village in East Anglia. I'm prepared to go there but don't expect to find much.'

'Something must be done. Whole thing has become a damned disaster.'

'Disaster?'

Camber leaned forward and his eyes bulged with the effort of mentally transfixing Samson with an arrow of such tragic importance that the fat detective would be shocked into sitting upright instead of lounging indolently in a swivel chair which squeaked as he swung from side to side. 'Caroline,' he said slowly, 'has been kidnapped. Whole damn shooting match has got completely out of control. Nobody knows where she is.'

'You're all on speaking terms again?'

Camber didn't like the question. 'Am with my daughter,' he replied gruffly. 'She's frantic with worry.'

'If Caroline has been kidnapped, it's a police matter. Has it been reported?'

'Certainly not.'

'Why not?'

'I'll show you why not.' Camber took out his spectacles and a piece of paper. After scanning the paper he handed it over. 'Read that.'

Samson read the letter aloud for the benefit of Shandy who was listening in the next room. When he had finished Camber said, 'Caro rang up Mabel yesterday afternoon. Sounded in high spirits. Intended coming home after having a meal with one of these crooks. Said she couldn't stick the other one. Fellow called Brown. My guess is that this "Mr X" and Brown are one and the same. May have given the slip to the other fellow, name of Hungerford. But I could be wrong. Perhaps it's Hungerford who's got her. What do you think?'

'Do Mr and Mrs Moore know you've come to see me?'

'Mabel does. Frank doesn't. She may tell him though. One thing certain. None of us will want the police in on this.'

Samson took a magnifying glass from a drawer and studied the envelope. 'The postmark is illegible, but I doubt if it would have helped much. Mr X isn't likely to have sent this from the place he's holding her, although it's almost axiomatic that if the most cunning of crooks is to be caught it will be invariably through him making the most foolish of mistakes.' He closed his eyes and reclined in his chair. It looked as though he was preparing to doze into sleep, but just as Camber was about to bang the desk with clenched fist he opened his eyes and said, 'We ought to put a tap on the Moores' phone in case a demand comes that way. I want everything recorded. I'd also like the fullest possible physical description of both men. I have a contact, an artist who often makes sketches for the police. I can bring him in. Would you ask Mr Moore to come and see me?'

Camber looked doubtful. 'Frank would shoot me if he knew I'd been to you.'

Samson gave a thin smile. 'But surely you've been shot at before, Colonel?'

Camber's moustache bristled. 'Of course I have. Not afraid of sticking out my neck.' He hesitated. 'There's one thing I should tell you.'

'Yes?'

'Caroline's past history. Didn't tell you any lies but didn't tell you the whole truth. May have made it look a bit one-sided. All Frank's fault and none of hers.'

Samson nodded. Any first-class detective worth his first-class fee knew perfectly well that faults were never entirely on one side.

'Bit of a problem child. I think that's the right description, although in the Army we used to say there were never bad soldiers only bad officers. Hate to have to talk like this. Sounds disloyal. But Caro was a destructive child. Mabel took her to a child-guidance psychiatrist. Told she and Frank should give much more love. Can't order love. Silly advice.' Camber cleared his throat as though the explanation was sticking in his gullet. 'Long and short of it is that she went off the rails when she was sixteeen. Dreadful time. Went missing for three weeks. Found in a caravan of a travelling fair. Had a couple of men with her. Don't want to go into details. No need to. Got rid of the baby at a private clinic. Scarred her. Hated her father for insisting she got rid of the baby. All very sordid. Another psychiatrist. Phoney profession, if you ask me. Said she had a psycho-something personality.'

'Psychopathic,' enquired Samson.

'Might have been. Anyway, thought I should tell you this. Could be useful background.'

Samson had stopped nodding but there was an implicit nod in his voice when he said, 'It is useful background. But with that sort of medical history it seems odd to commit her to the care of two male deprogrammers.'

'Couldn't agree with you more. My view entirely. That's why I was so damn angry when I found out how I'd been tricked to get her out of the clutches of one man only to put her into the hands of two quacks.' Camber sat very erect. 'Feel completely vindicated,' he added.

Samson picked up the letter. 'I'd like to get this photocopied.'

'All right.'

Samson pressed the button on his desk. Shandy, who knew before she was summoned, that she was wanted to make a copy of a document, entered the room with notebook and pencil in hand as though expecting to take some dictated instructions. The client would have no idea that she'd heard every word. Samson observed the little subtlety and as he asked her to make the necessary copy he gazed at her midriff. Earlier he had suggested that she was more interested in this case than in most because she identified with Caroline in some way. Shandy had denied this, but after hearing of Caroline's visit to an abortion clinic she would surely feel sympathy, if not a measure of identification. Women, in Samson's opinion, were liable to perk up eagerly when the word 'baby' was mentioned. It had much the same trigger response as saying 'Walk' to a dog.

Turning to Camber, he said, 'Will you ask Mr Moore to give me a call?'

'I'll have to make an apology or two first. Called him some hard names. Still, a man's not a man who can't swallow his pride. But if he won't get in touch with you, and I doubt if he will' – Camber peered at Samson as though trying to read a prompt-card – 'will you carry on acting for me?'

'Naturally. And don't worry. Things may not be as bad as they seem.'

Camber jerked back as though the prompt-card had exploded in his face. 'Not as bad as they seem! Couldn't be much worse. Why do you say that?'

'I'll show you when my secretary comes back.'

A few moments later he handed Camber the photo-copy and kept the original letter for himself.

'Look at the writing, Colonel. What strikes you about it?'

The spectacles came out again. They gave Camber a slightly owlish look.

'Nothing strikes me. It's her writing all right. Recognise it at once.'

'Quite neat,' observed Samson. 'Words well spaced. Margins level and the message exactly fills the paper. There's no cramping. It's almost as though she knew in advance precisely what she was going to write.'

'That's true. What are you driving at, Samson?'

'And examine the bit where she writes about her fingers being cut off one by one. The script doesn't falter. And yet one might expect, in the act of writing which is essentially one for the fingers, she would be very conscious of the threat. But the curves of "f" and "g" are unflurried.' Samson rose to his feet. 'Leave it with me. I'll be in touch.'

He held the photograph of Caroline in one hand and the letter in the other and gazed at each in turn. Shandy, who had just brought him a mug of strong Indian tea, a ham sandwich and a slab of fruit cake, said, 'Trying to fill out the silhouette?'

'Yes. I'm getting a picture. But it's still pretty hazy. I wonder if we could get a few enlightening touches from my old friend, Marcus Wayne.'

'That con-man Casanova!'

'He's always played it straight with me,' said Samson.

'And so he should. It was thanks to you he got a Queen's Pardon . . . Do you want an analysis done?'

'See if he's free and if he is take a taxi there.' He handed her the letter. 'Tell him it's urgent. I don't want what he calls an in-depth analysis. Just a broad outline; a graphological lightning sketch.'

She smiled and patted her stomach. 'This should make me safe.'

'Don't count on it,' replied Samson lugubriously, 'but I reckon you're capable of repelling all boarders as we used to say in the Navy. As we used to say? By God, the style is infectious. Must have caught it from Camber. Damn silly. What?'

Shandy shook her head. 'You're a lovely detective, Samson, but a dead-loss mimic . . . See you.'

Dear old Sammy,

Distracted as I am by the presence of the beauteous Elaine, even more lovely in her present delicate condition, herewith a snap appraisal of a missive which to sharper eyes than mine might betray criminal intent.

We have an odd dish here. Highly imaginative, intuitive and impressionable, she is also only a mite less hard than the diamond set in a platinum ring worn by the beauteous Elaine. I doubt if she is good at forming relationships (like me!) as she is probably on one long ego trip (again like yours truly!).

Her lower zone, graphologically-speaking, is a dead

giveaway. S–M tendencies very strong. Probably the accent on the M. But if she invites sexual abuse she also undoubtedly controls the degree of abuse. In addition I would say our Caroline (if that's her real name) is arrogant, prideful, unforgiving, and a right bitch if crossed.

If she is your intended, my dear old Sammy, take my advice and don't marry her. On second thoughts, with a wife like her a man would lose weight quicker than on any diet. Maybe she'd do you good.

Impertinence comes, as usual, with deepest respect.

Your old friend – although some scurrilous scribbler once called me a man without friends,

Marcus

'You really must get another suit,' said Shandy brushing his coat vigorously with a clothes brush. 'There's a shop in the Edgware Road just for fellows like you.'

'Fat slobs?'

'Outsize chunks of manhood.'

Samson chuckled. 'Do you think I should marry and lose weight?'

'Happily married men put it on. Paul has.'

She gave the contented smile of a woman who knows how to please the man she loves. Her smile was lost on Samson who didn't care for the clothes brushing routine which she insisted on before he left the office for the day. It made him feel like a tatty-coated horse at the mercy of an over-conscientious groom.

'We've got to keep you looking trim,' she went on. 'Prospective secretaries are going to assess you as much as you'll be assessing them. You can't have a brilliant girl turn you down because of your appearance.'

'Have things got so progressive, egalitarian, enlightened and utterly ridiculous that it's the employees who hire the employer?'

'More or less.'

'You're probably right if that report I had to make on company security against petty pilfering is anything to go by.'

She hung up the brush. 'That'll do. Now then, before we go, tell me. Spill the beans. Ever since you read Marcus's letter you've been grinning like a banana.'

'It's only a hunch.'

'We share hunches, don't we?'

He shifted from foot to foot as though diffident about the value of his hunch; it was a show of elephantine coyness. 'Oh, all right,' he said at length. 'While you were away I boned up on some textbooks, particularly Sargant's *Battle for the Mind*. If I understand it aright, the person easiest to brainwash is the hearty extravert and the most difficult is the mentally unstable or the psychopath.'

'In other words Caroline wouldn't be a walk-over either to programme or deprogramme?'

'Right. And her handwriting was careful; not the writing of someone under intense pressure. And now we have Marcus's independent opinion. His insight about her being the sort who can control the degree of her abuse by others could be right.'

While he was talking she slipped on her pink rainproof and picked up a plastic carrier-bag filled with groceries. 'And your hunch,' she said, 'is that there's something phoney about that letter?'

He smiled benignly. 'Well done.'

'Don't patronise. The next girl might not take it as well as I do.' She moved out into a narrow corridor and waited while Samson locked up. 'Are you walking, taking a bus or a cab?' she asked.

'It's a fine evening. I'll walk. Take you to the bus-stop. And don't forget. Early to bed tonight. We've got a busy day tomorrow and I want to make an early start.'

They walked down some steps and into the street.

'I hope it's not foggy,' she said. 'I don't fancy a foggy day in the fens.'

'I don't fancy a day there at all.' He sighed. 'But we'd better sniff around, although I'm sure the scent will be cold, if ever there's been a scent.'

A group of youths who looked like riders in search of stray motor-cycles came down the pavement. Other pedestrians moved clear, but Samson sailed straight on after tucking Shandy behind him so that he was a battleship leading a corvette. The bunch of youths parted like a wave before the prow of a dreadnought, and re-formed when Samson had passed. One called out 'Fat-arse' but it was a taunt he blandly ignored.

An Asian who was pulling down shutters over a fruit shop said, 'Good evening, Mr Samson.'

' 'Evening, Mr Patel. The melon was delicious.' He turned to Shandy. 'I didn't tell you, but while you were being chatted up by our favourite philandering graphologist I got a call from Mr Frank Moore.'

'No good?'

'A rude man. He told me to mind my own business. What an unreasonable thing to say.'

She laughed lightly. 'Is it? Did he say anything else?'

'He had the nerve to tell me that I had no right to meddle in something which concerned parents and their child. I had to remind him that Caroline was no longer a child in the custodial care of her parents. He didn't like that and after a few impolite words he rang off.'

They arrived at the bus-stop and joined a small queue.

'So you didn't get any sort of description of Brown or Hungerford?'

'That doesn't matter too much. It's a picture of Caroline I'm trying to build up. In this particular case *cherchez la femme* has a dual meaning.'

'And I don't suppose you got any information on where they were holding her before the thing became a kidnapping. I'll bet it was a cottage near Fen Soken.'

'Well, tomorrow we might find out.' Samson gave a smile as pink as her coat. 'Here's your bus. Take care of yourself.'

'Don't worry. I'm going to ride in it, not lift it.'

CHAPTER ELEVEN

They drove through country where straggling villages were separated by flat tracts of hedgeless fields, occasionally seeing a disused windmill or passing close to wartime airfields where old concrete runways sliced across furrows of ploughed earth.

Shandy looked at the map on her lap. 'Three miles to go,' she said.

Samson, who hadn't spoken for some time except in grunts and monosyllables, said, 'I'd hate to be driving along here in bad weather and have something go wrong with the car.'

'It's a lovely day, so that's not likely to happen. Your trouble is that you're coming here against your will. You think it'll be a waste of time.'

'I wish you wouldn't keep on using that expression, Shandy. You might as well say a waste of atoms for all the sense it makes.'

'Time isn't atoms,' she replied.

'Oh yes it is. The latest theory is that Time has an atomic or granular structure and its minimum spatial displacement corresponds to the diameter of a proton. The minimum time to cross this infinitesimally tiny distance is called a chronon. Time is chronons strung together like pearls on a necklace.'

'You've just given Miller's "String of Pearls" a new dimension. And all right. This journey isn't a waste of time, but it might be a waste of energy. Does that suit you better?'

'Much better. It appeals to my inherent laziness. So do these roads. Dead straight. Easy driving.'

They didn't speak again until he pulled up in the centre of the village. It had a wide main street which in more prosperous times had been used as a market-place. Samson parked his car near a small county library which was closed. Switching off the engine he said, 'Well, get cracking. Let's see what you can do.'

'Me? What about you?'

'I'm going to read the paper. I need to catch up with world news.'

'So I'm expected to do the nosing around on my own?'

'This is your party, Shandy. I don't want to steal your glory. You were the one smart enough to find out about Hungerford and where he had a cottage. Don't you want to see it through?'

'What about my delicate condition?'

Samson patted her knee affectionately. 'You know that your condition troubles me least when you're doing something for me. Look at it this way. Country people are always suspicious of strangers. A big, ungainly creature like me won't get anywhere with locals unless it's in a pub and the pubs aren't open yet. You, on the other hand, will attract sympathy. Country people can identify with simple things like crop rotation and pregnancy.'

'Thanks very much. I feel like a cow in calf.'

'Good. You've got the idea. Exploit your tummy.'

She shook her head. 'I pity my successor,' she said, reaching for the door handle.

Samson picked up *The Times* and began reading the foreign news. But as soon as Shandy was out of sight he lowered the paper and became lost in thought. Theories and philosophies about Time fascinated him. Is eternity cyclic and endlessly repetitive or is it linear and infinitely continuous? Is Time destructive, as medieval scholars thought, when they used symbols of hour-glass and scythe; or creative, as those scientists who advance theories of Time preceding the Big Bang suggest? Does it have religious significance, as a heretical sect of Zoroastrians believe, or is it a succession of fleeting opportunities to be taken on the wing by hedonists?

But the question which preoccupied Samson was whether he had put across the theory of atomised Time to Shandy. The disturbing fact was that although he could put forward the theory he didn't really comprehend it. To a practical man such measurements as a million millionth part of a million millionth part of a second – a chronon – were so hypothetical as to be impossible to envisage.

He was still thinking of Time when she returned.

'It's my turn to say "Get cracking".'

He switched on the engine. 'Where to?'

She looked smug. 'Straight on through the village. Take the fourth turning on the left where there's an old milestone. Then go for a mile. Turn right and travel along a track which is a sort of causeway. Straight ahead, and a mile further on, there's a cottage. It belongs to a man called Fastnet. He bought it from Stephen Hungerford and sometimes rents it back to Hungerford and other friends and acquaintances. Hungerford was seen two or three days ago. He was driving a blue van. How's that?'

'Not bad,' said Samson negotiating the wheel so that he steered clear of an awkwardly parked horse-box.

' "Not bad" being litotes for absolutely spectacular.'

Samson accelerated. 'How did you come by this information?'

'Simple. I went to a general store and asked for some aspirins. Said I had a headache but perhaps that was because I'd been travelling and on account of my condition. The old dear who ran the shop was easy to chat to. I only had to say I was at Girton at the same time as a chap called Stephen Hungerford was up at university, and I believed he lived in these parts, to get it all.'

'Not bad at all . . . You don't really have a headache?'

'Of course not.'

The village ended in an estate of ugly new yellow-brick council houses which seemed out of harmony with the older red-brick terrace houses and the expanding field of cabbage.

'That'll be where the foreigners live,' said Shandy. 'They call it Colditz.'

'Which foreigners?'

'East-end Londoners who have given up hope of finding a home in the big city. They don't get much of a welcome from the locals.'

'You seem to have learned a lot,' said Samson.

'It was my pregnancy that did the trick but the aspirins helped. The foreigners are great customers for aspirins and anything else that claims to relieve tension or headaches.'

'The poor devils are probably riddled with psychosomatic illnesses. Thank God I don't live here,' said Samson feelingly. 'Start keeping your eyes peeled for that milestone.'

Within ten minutes they had reached the track which ran along a high bank between fields. A short way along the track was a notice, 'Private property – No access.' The terrain changed. They were still travelling above flat land but the fields had given way to marshy ground, and sedges and rushes had taken over the arable farmland.

Samson came to a stop outside the cottage almost exactly where Brown's body had been loaded on the van. He and Shandy got out of the car and looked around. 'Recent tyre marks,' he said, peering at the ground.

She shivered slightly and pulled her coat round her shoulders. 'I wouldn't like to be here when a winter wind is blowing. The cottage doesn't look occupied, does it?' He took a bunch of keys out of his overcoat pocket. 'Let's investigate.'

'Breaking and entering, Samson? That's naughty.'

'Entering only if nobody answers the door-bell.'

Once inside the cottage they moved around checking each room. Samson sniffed like a bloodhound trying to capture the odorous traces of humanity and cooked food. He examined the waste-disposal bin and checked ledges for dust. His eyes, normally hooded and sleepy, flickered everywhere adding a stream of messages to his sensory input. Shandy, who had seen him behave like this before, stood with a slightly amused smile tilting the corners of her mouth. It was his habit, after acting like some anthropoid geiger counter, to come out with a stunningly obvious deduction which, after she had dutifully laughed, he might follow with something shrewd.

After combing the rooms he ended in the lounge and sat heavily in an armchair.

'Well,' she asked.

'This place could have been used to deprogramme some-one.'

'Incredible. How can you possibly know that?'

'By using logic to arrive at the conclusion that there are a sufficient number of rooms for technicians and victim to be separate when necessary.'

She clapped her hands. 'Brilliant!'

'Thank you.'

'Now let's have the less clever stuff.'

'I'd say that whoever was here has left within the last couple of days but I'll tell you what really interests me.'

'Yes?'

'Just look around you. Caroline must have put up one hell of a struggle before they got her out.'

She nodded. 'I thought the same. It's all so tidy. But look what I found while you were nosing round the bathroom.'

She produced a writing-pad which she'd been holding behind her back.

'It looks like the paper she used to write the letter,' said Samson. 'And now see what I've found.' He pulled out a handkerchief, opened it carefully and extracted strands of auburn hair. 'From the bathroom plug-hole,' he explained.

'They cut her hair while she was having a bath?' Shandy pulled a face. 'I don't like the idea of that.'

Samson put the hairs back in his handkerchief. 'It's more likely that she was made to stand in the bath so that they could wash away any hairs they didn't collect. Or she might have been given scissors and told to cut her own hair.' He tore a page from the writing-pad. 'We'll keep this for comparison purposes.'

'What now,' she asked.

'The dustbin outside. Dustbins, trash-cans, call them what you will, they are marvellous repositories of information. I once had the contents of a dust-bin listed one by one and some of them chemically analysed. There were three hundred and twelve items and I found traces of four people; two men and two women. This gave the lie to the house owner who said he'd been absolutely alone for a fortnight.'

'Another missing-person case?'

He gave a wry look. 'What else? The wife had disappeared. What I hadn't been told until I presented my client with the evidence was that she had disappeared after a swap party. He couldn't face the fact that she'd run away with a casual swap partner. There had to be some other reason.'

As he locked the front door he said, 'I hope you wiped everything you touched.'

'I did.'

'You're a woman in a million, Shandy. If only . . .'

'If only, Samson.'

He gave a shrug of such magnitude it might have been an impersonation of an elephant struggling into an overcoat. 'Let's look at that dustbin,' he said.

Among the detritus they found empty whisky bottles. 'Heavy drinkers, these technicians,' said Samson. 'Or one of them is. Cheap blended stuff. Maybe he drinks for the effect rather than the taste. Perhaps he's got things to forget.'

'Like women?'

'Women. Or unfulfilled ambitions. Or even himself.'

He was driving in bottom gear and scanning each side of the track. Suddenly he braked.

'A clue?' she asked.

'Don't mock an honest man trying to do an honest job.

Instead, tell me why someone should want to drive off this apology for a road. Was it a stampede of frogs coming from the opposite direction?'

He switched off the engine and they got out of the car. 'Let's see where these lead,' he said.

They followed the tracks which had been made by the van until these stopped at a point where the ground became soggy. Broken reeds led them to a place where, between tussocks of tall marsh grasses, there was a patch of muddy water.

Samson looked around. 'Nothing here,' he said. 'But what a good place to lose something you don't want.' As he spoke the muddy water seemed to shiver.

'Did you see that,' she said. 'It moved.'

Samson didn't reply. He was crouching down and gingerly extracting something which stood out at a sharp angle and had been concealed by rushes. When he got it clear he wiped it on some grass. The face of Richard Wagner was revealed.

'It's a record sleeve,' said Shandy. 'Who'd want to throw away a record?'

'That's something for us to think about on the way home,' he replied.

Conjecture led nowhere. Musical appreciation was not one of Samson's accomplishments but he could think of no good reason to throw away a long-playing record of excerpts from *Tristan and Isolde* unless it had been stolen and the thief, suffering from remorse or guilt, had wanted to rid himself of the disc. It might be that other things had been swallowed up in the mire but any salvage operation would require proper equipment and Samson had no intention of hiring a contractor to scoop up mud on private property.

The Wagner sleeve would have to remain an unsolved mystery for the time being.

'I had no idea you were a whisky snob,' said Shandy, out of the blue.

'What do you mean?'

'It was the way you said "Cheap blended stuff." '

Deprived of his usual high-calorie, high-cholesterol intake Samson became tetchy and irritable. 'I speak what I think,' he said shortly. 'It was cheap blended stuff and I said so. Don't infer snobbery from that.'

They continued the journey in silence. Shandy was glad when they finally arrived back at the office late in the afternoon.

As a matter of routine she checked the answer-phone service. There were three messages. It was the third which made Samson forget pangs of hunger and delayed her departure for home. The message was from Colonel Camber. It said, 'I must see you as soon as possible. Please contact me at my home number. My daughter has received a ransom demand for one hundred thousand pounds. Failure to deliver will result in Caro's death.'

'No, sir,' said Camber, his neck flushing and his back poker-rigid, 'I am not on speaking terms with my son-in-law. Happily I enjoy the confidence of my daughter, and in reply to your second question, my son-in-law has no intention of going to the police.'

Samson shook his head. 'As I suspected. A man with little judgment or common sense. Now, how exactly was this second message received?'

Camber relaxed slightly. 'Phone call. From Caro herself. Spoke to her mother. Said something like, "Hello,

Mummy. I'm speaking with a gun in my back. Tell my father to get a hundred thousand pounds in used five-pound notes together. Wrap them securely in something completely waterproof. Further instructions will follow. If you don't do exactly as I say I shall be killed." And then she rang off. You can imagine how Mabel felt. Very, very distressing.'

'Does your grand-daughter like Wagner?' asked Samson.

Camber was taken aback. 'Wagner? Not to my knowledge.'

'Do you know anyone who does?'

'Wagner? The composer? Not my cup of tea. Prefer military music, naturally. Like Vera Lynn too. Why?'

Samson toyed with a paper-knife. 'A shot in the dark, he said. 'On a different tack, would you say your grand-daughter was easily led?'

Camber considered the question. 'Yes. Led astray by fairground oafs. Led astray by this Irving man.'

Samson balanced the paper-knife on a fat forefinger. 'Let's take the fairground people. You won't like what I'm going to say but it's important. She was found living with men in a caravan. Right?'

Camber took a deep breath. 'Correct.'

'Would you say that she was the plaything of these men or more like the queen of a male harem?'

'Really, Samson! Is this necessary?'

'I think so.' Samson raised his eyelids. 'Well?'

'Plaything or queen? Can't see that it has anything whatsoever to do with the case. But queen. Yes, without a doubt.' Camber paused. 'And yet. I don't know. Very odd business. Unwholesome.'

'The next bit,' said Samson, 'should be easier. I want you

to talk about Caroline for as long as you can. I'll stay here till midnight if needs be. I want to know everything about her. No detail is too trivial.'

'How can that help?'

'I'm trying to understand her,' said Samson gently. 'The understanding of a person is often the solution to a problem relating to that person.'

A little more than three hours later and after Camber had gone, Samson said, 'It's been a long day. Are you sure you want to stay on?'

'I've been on the phone to Paul. He's getting his own meal. And I want to be in on this. I've become personally involved.'

'I knew it. In that cottage I could see you imagining what it would be like if it was you having your hair cut. I really ought to send you home.'

'Not a chance.'

'In that case how about slipping out and getting me a takeaway from the Golden Bamboo?'

She shook her head emphatically. 'If I can't get my husband a meal I'm damned if I'm getting you one . . . What do you make of it, Samson?'

The detective stripped a cigar of cellophane wrapping and held it to his ear. 'You overheard everything?'

'Yes.'

'Most of it sounded typical of a wilful and rather neurotic child. An attention-seeker on a grand scale and a dedicated defier of authority, parental and otherwise. I lost count of the schools she ran away from or played truant at. Two or three things struck me as particularly interesting.' He lighted the cigar. 'First, her love of parties when she was smaller and her favourite party game. Camber remembered that clearly. He sometimes played it with her when there was no one else around.'

'Hide-and-seek.'

'Yes. Hide-and-seek. It flashed through my mind that some children's games symbolise adult life-styles. Most children's games of enduring popularity contain situations applicable to the world of grown-ups. You get my point?'

Samson's eyes were two rifles drawing beads on her.

'Hide-and-seek is Caroline's life-style?'

'Does that sound far-fetched,' he asked.

'I don't see what you're driving at apart from the obvious idea that she might contrive disappearance so as to be found. But she didn't contrive being abducted by deprogramming merchants, so where does that get you?'

'What about the time she hid in the cupboard under the stairs? It was the last place Camber looked for her because he knew she was frightened of this particular place. He didn't dream she'd ever go into it voluntarily.'

'You're thinking aloud and using me as a sounding board.'

'That's right, and a very pretty sounding board you make.'

She shook her head. 'I may have moments of beauty at certain angles and in the half-light, but pretty I am not. Now let me get you an ash-tray. I hate it when you get ash all down your front. It makes you look . . .' She didn't finish, but went to fetch a heavy onyx dish.

After he had deposited ash he said, 'Another thing which nags at my mind is relativity.'

She slumped into a chair.

'Fascinating subject,' he continued. 'What we owe to

Einstein. I only wish philosophers would devise a theory of human relativity.'

'You've lost me,' she said wearily.

'I'm thinking of the bit Camber found so distasteful. Is the girl who sleeps with a lot of men a tramp or is she an earth mother who use men's desires to enslave them? She could be either. It depends entirely on your standpoint. It's all a matter of relativity.'

Shandy laughed. 'I like it. Use men's desires to enslave them. I've missed my vocation.'

'Does the group use the groupie or does the groupie use the group?'

'Right.'

'So some people can appear to be manipulated while doing some manipulation themselves.'

'And Caroline is a manipulator?'

Samson took his cigar from his mouth too quickly and ash sprayed down the front of his coat. Shandy said nothing but rolled her eyes to the ceiling.

'I'm not saying she's a manipulator,' he replied, brushing his front with his hand, 'but I don't see her as a forlorn little waif.'

'You were doing well with groupie but words like waif date you.'

'Another thing that puzzles me is why the ransom should be wrapped in something waterproof. Is it to be dropped in a river or the sea?'

'I've no idea,' said Shandy.

'She's supposed to have a morbid fear of drowning. The technicians know this. Are they holding her in some place surrounded by water?'

She jerked forward in her seat. 'I think you've hit on something.'

Samson smiled complacently. 'Or has she gone some-where surrounded by water. Is she hiding in the cupboard under the stairs once more?'

'Where does her father keep his boat?'

'That,' said Samson, 'is something I neglected to ask the good colonel. Put a call through to him. He should be home by now.'

CHAPTER TWELVE

Sharp scatters of rain fell from sky-borne galleons of clouds which raced from the sea as if searching for an inland anchorage which would spare them from the whipping east wind. In a chill dusk a lighted buoy flashed out of deepening greyness giving the assurance of landfall to the crew of a battered rusty coaster which laboured its way through the shallows and shoals which lay between sea and river mouth. The long flat grey coastline was stippled with a succession of broken wave crests and, apart from the coaster carrying a cargo of timber from Norway, not another ship under steam or sail could be seen.

Once past the buoy the coaster moved into quieter waters. Ahead and to starboard the warm lights of a town twinkled in the distance, and in a nearby creek some moored yachts rocked gently as the swell from the ship's bows reached them. Inside one of the yachts the sound of a mooring ring clanking against its pole could be heard.

'What was that?' asked Stephen.

Caroline gave a brief laugh. 'Don't be so nervous.'

'I don't like it here.'

'You don't like being afloat,' she asked smoothly.

'I wish we hadn't come.'

'We have. So relax.'

They were inside the cabin of her father's ketch. It had

been easy to break open the padlock fastening the cabin door and they were now sitting on the bunks waiting for a pan of water to boil.

'You'll feel better after a hot drink,' she said.

'I don't feel bad. It's just that I don't feel right.'

'Why not?'

He shook his head. 'Don't know. Out of my element, maybe.'

'It's the same for me.'

They were sitting opposite each other. She had changed into a thick-knit red sweater and brushed denim jeans, and on her feet she wore white rubber boots. He sat with his arms crossed and his hands tucked under his armpits as if trying to keep warm.

'I thought you didn't like the water,' he said. 'I thought you were afraid of drowning.'

'My parents told you that?'

'Well, yes.'

A look of cat-like satisfaction creamed her face. 'I never gave them the pleasure of knowing. My father would have thought he'd done it, but I did it myself.'

'Did what?'

'I hated sailing and I was terrified of drowning but without them knowing I learned to swim, and I learned to face my fears, and what had once been an ordeal wasn't an ordeal any more. But I never let them know.'

'You're not afraid of drowning?'

'I'm not saying that. I'm not completely cured. When you left me on my own in that marsh I was in a state of complete panic. All the old fears came to the surface. Why did you do it?'

He lowered his head. 'It was my job.' His voice was sulkily apologetic.

'It was your job to terrify a helpless woman?'

'I'm sorry. I said I was sorry on our way down.'

'All right. I suppose it's past history. Tomorrow we'll take the boat out.'

His head jerked up. 'What?'

'Take the boat out. It's part of the plan.'

'I don't understand.'

'You don't have to. I'm in charge now.'

'I thought we were partners.'

'We are. But I'm in charge. You want the money, don't you?'

'I want the thousand I'm owed.'

'You wouldn't say no to a hundred thousand.'

He shifted uneasily on the bunk and gave a false laugh. 'What are you trying to do? Make me into a criminal?'

'You already are. You're guilty of abduction and false imprisonment. But I'm not going to hold it against you. Come over here.'

She reached out into the space between them. He unfolded his arms and took her hand. Gently but firmly she pulled him towards her.

The boat rocked almost imperceptibly on an ebbing tide. It was dark inside the cabin.

'I told you,' she said patiently, 'when we were back at the cottage. If my father pays up it proves he really cares.'

'And then you'll go back home?'

'Of course.' After a silence, she added, 'You don't seem happy about something.'

'You say it'll prove your father cares if he hands over a ransom, but also you could be doing it to score over him. A sort of revenge.'

They were lying on their sides, facing each other, on one of the bunks.

'It's nice being confined like this with you,' she said, 'but imagine what it must have been like on a slave-trader's ship.'

'I wish when you called your mother you hadn't said there was a gun in your back.'

'It heightens the drama.'

'Is that what this is to you? Drama?'

In the darkness she made the sound of someone sighing wearily. 'You've got to get out of the habit of trying to interrogate me. It's tedious. Anyway, we've got your gun with us.'

'That's a long-barrelled shot-gun. You gave the impression a revolver was being jabbed in your back. It may be just the thing that makes them go to the police, and then we'd be in trouble.'

'If they go to the police they'll be disobeying my instructions and I'll know they don't care, and I won't go back. But if they obey, I will. And you'll get your money.'

'You said your father would withhold it. Laugh in my face.'

'Stephen,' she said sharply, 'you aren't really a fool so don't talk like one. We'll get the money, deduct what's due to you and I'll take the rest home . . . Unless you want it for your projects.' She nuzzled against him and kissed the tip of his nose.

'Don't tempt me.' He shifted slightly to ease an arm that was growing numb. 'I've got a clean reputation and I want it to stay that way.'

'Snatching people and trying to brainwash them out of their beliefs is clean,' she enquired.

'It's not brainwashing. It's deprogramming. It's restoring normality to the abnormal.'

'A good work. Charitable.'

'At least it's not the sort of charitable Eventide Joy is.'

'That's true.'

'Caroline?'

'Yes.'

'This man. Irving O. What does O stand for?'

'Old.'

'You've been rescued from a dangerous paranoiac. You do realise that?'

'Oh, I do. You carried me away like a Barry Sheene on a thousand c.c. supercharged Japanese motor-bike.'

'Don't laugh at me.'

'I'm not. But why do you feel the need to justify what you do?'

He didn't answer and in a long silence the mooring ring rattled against the pole. This was followed by a mournful sound from the far distance.

'What was that,' he asked nervously.

'A ship's siren. You are jumpy. Relax.'

'Caroline?'

'I'm getting sleepy.'

'Just one question.'

'What?'

'Irving. You didn't really find him attractive, did you?'

'Yes. But I don't any more. Now go to sleep.'

'I wish you'd tell me what the next move is,' he said petulantly over a breakfast of boiled eggs and buttered toast.

'I call home and tell them to deliver the money.'

'Where?'

'To a derelict pill-box on Mersea Island. It's part of the

wartime defences which haven't been cleared. There are no houses near. It's deserted. Isolated.'

'That's not far from here, is it?'

'Quite close. We'll go out soon and prospect the area from the sea.'

Stephen ground the empty egg-shell to fragments with his spoon. The action helped to express what he felt. 'But I'm supposed to be holding *you* hostage. Why the hell should I come to a place your family know well? It doesn't make sense. They'll suspect something is fishy.'

'You aren't holding me. Brown is. Remember? And let them think what they want. If anything goes wrong it's proof that we weren't really serious. I'll take the blame and you'll be in the clear.'

He shook his head. 'It's so damned amateur.'

'And you're so professional?'

'At least I brought you to your senses. I brought you back to normal.'

They were facing each other over a small table rigged between the bunks. She turned away her head. Light from the cabin lamp caught the reddish sheen of her cropped hair and cast a shadow in a cheek hollow. She looked young and vulnerable. He reached out to stroke her hair.

'No,' she said, pulling away her head.

He withdrew his hand. 'All right. We'll play it your way. When are you going to make this call?'

She stood up and peered through a porthole. 'It's a good thing there are waterproofs aboard. It's raining out and the cloud is low. It's like a fine mist.'

'You don't intend sailing to wherever we're going?'

'Not likely. We'll use the motor.'

'You know how to work it?'

She gave a contemptuous look. 'Understanding engines

isn't an exclusively male talent.'

'I didn't mean that.'

'What did you mean if it wasn't that women aren't expected to know about engines?'

He gazed at the crumpled egg-shell and said nothing for a few moments. Then he asked, 'Do you want me to come with you to the phone box?'

'No. You stay here. I'll check that the van's all right. I shan't be long.' She gave him a long, analytical look, her eyes resting on the bomber-jacket which he had buttoned to the neck against the cold. 'You'd better wear my father's oilskins. You'll find them in that hatch. And put on his sweater too. It'll be very cold once we leave this creek and move into the river and you look half-frozen already.'

When she had gone he looked for the sweater and oilskins and put them on. Except for the calor-gas stove there was no heating on board and the river chill had seeped into his bones. He wished he had never come to this damp, grey place on the edge of the bleak North Sea.

Ever since burying Brown he had felt that events were controlling him and he was powerless to stop them. It was as though he had suddenly become a passenger in a car which he had been driving a split second before. But now he was in the passenger seat and the car was travelling fast into a belt of thickening fog and he was unable to reach the brake pedal.

He noticed his gun propped beneath the echo-sounder and decided to check that the cartridges hadn't become damp in the river air. After doing this he sat on a bunk and began polishing the barrels with a rag. He was very fond of this gun which had once belonged to his grand-father, a gamekeeper. Its wooden stock had a deep rich

131

glow which comes from years of polishing and the metal by the trigger guard was beautifully chased. As he handled the gun he thought of the fens and wished he was out wildfowling.

In some ways the flat coastline was reminiscent of fen country; one seemed to be a natural geophysical extension of the other; and yet he felt out of his element and uncomfortable. If mankind were divided between land-lovers and sea-lovers he would have been deeply entrenched on land. It wasn't that he disliked water and wetness; it was more that the sea represented instability and volatile emotions – aspects of himself which he feared – and the land symbolised security.

In the boat his sense of security was somehow threatened. It wasn't simply that he found the environment vaguely hostile; reason told him that Caroline's plan was foolish. He didn't believe her father would willingly pay over a ransom; and, if no ransom were forthcoming, what would the next move be? They couldn't spend the winter on the boat, but where would they go? He didn't want to take her back to his flat in London and yet he didn't want to lose her.

Full of uncertainty and wishing he could extricate himself from the situation he'd allowed himself to be manoeuvred into he put away the gun, propping it under the echo-sounder, and stooped his way on to the deck. Visibility was poor and a fine mesh of rain blurred contours and dulled colours. There was no sign of life on the other moored ships except for the furthest where a man was working on repairs to a mast.

Then he heard the chug of an engine and a few moments later a motor launch appeared. It was making its way purposefully towards the sea and the word 'Police' stood out in large letters on its cabin. He glimpsed a couple of men in white sweaters before ducking his head in the pretence that he needed to adjust the fastenings of a rope. The launch soon disappeared from sight but it had been an unpleasant reminder that the law operated on water as well as on land.

He went back into the cabin. She had been gone only half an hour but it seemed like many hours. Why should I worry? he thought. I'm not a child. I don't depend on her for anything. When she gets back I'll tell her I'm through with this charade. I'll offer her a lift to her home and if she refuses I'll leave her. I have other things to do. Ambitions to be fulfilled. Let others fight the manipulators. I've had enough. My life is elsewhere.

He heard her voice. 'I'm back,' she called.

She entered the cabin and pulled down the hood of her waterproof anorak. Her friendly smile, followed by a quick kiss on the cheek, made his heart sink. It wasn't going to be easy to finish their relationship.

'Caroline, I've been thinking.'

'You have?'

'I'm not going through with this.'

Her face fell. 'Why not? They've agreed. Don't you want your fee? Don't you want me to go back to my parents?'

'Of course I do. I'll take you there. Let's drop this crazy ransom business.'

Her face seemed to narrow. 'It wasn't crazy yesterday.'

'Maybe not, but I've been thinking . . .'

She threw up her hands. 'My God! The man's been thinking. Move over, Plato. Okay, if you want to think I'll give you something to think about. If you don't see this through I swear I'll bring charges of forcible abduction and rape. Multiple rape. I'll go to the police and tell them I

133

was raped at gunpoint and made to blackmail my parents with ransom demands.'

He looked horrified and tried to speak but she interrupted. If she had been a cat her back would have been arched and she would have been spitting.

'Shut up! Let me finish. If it's your story against mine there isn't a court in the land which wouldn't believe my story against yours. And so, Stephen darling, you'll play it my way. Right?'

'I thought . . .'

'Thought! Thinking!' She gave a contemptuous laugh. 'That's the trouble with you. You can't manage your own thoughts so you try to foul up other people's. By what right do you go around twisting other people's thoughts? Giving it a do-gooding name doesn't make it less dirty than it is.'

He was now looking as if he had been slapped sharply across his face and the pain in his cheek had spread to his eyes. He tried to speak but choked on the words.

Suddenly she was in his arms. 'I'm sorry,' she said. 'I didn't mean to blow my top. I do love you.' She kissed him on the mouth and pulled away smiling.

He felt very confused.

'It's all lined up,' she said gleefully. 'I spoke to Mother. Father was away. He had some urgent meeting he couldn't cancel. The old story. But she says the money is ready and will be delivered tomorrow to wherever we want. Naturally I made out I was speaking under pressure. Someone in the booth with me. I said that Father must go with the money to a hotel in Colchester and wait for further instructions. If there was any attempt at a double-cross I'd be killed.'

He shook his head.

'Stop looking so miserable. We've got work to do.'

'What work?'

'We're going to Mersea Island to check that pill-box is still available. It's two years since I was last there.'

'How do we go?'

'By sea.'

'In this? Sailing?'

She laughed. 'Don't look so anguished. Of course I'm not sailing. We'll go under power. Now move over. There are things to be turned on like petrol, electrics and the sea-cock.'

'Please listen to me, Caroline.'

She paused and regarded him seriously. 'No. I spent days listening to you at that godforsaken cottage. Remember? Now it's your turn to do the listening. There's a life-jacket under that seat. Put it on.'

'You must listen,' he pleaded. 'While you were away a police launch came by. What would they want?'

She smiled. 'They're after people like you and me, darling. People who break into yachts. There are a lot of thieves around.'

'What if they see us?'

'What if they do? We're just out on a pleasure trip. Where's your sense of adventure?'

'I think I've lost it,' he said sadly. 'Like I've lost other things.'

She made no reply but busied herself fixing the gear lever.

He donned the life-jacket.

She pressed the starter button and the two-stroke engine burst into life.

Blurred with rain, the coastline was like a thin strip of sodden driftwood washed ashore by a murky grey-green sea. A south-east wind scoured the surface of restless water creating white-splinter wave-crests before it hurried inland over the Essex countryside.

Stephen huddled by the cabin, oilskins buttoned up to his chin. 'How much further,' he called, raising his voice to a shout, although she was sitting only a few feet away holding the tiller.

'We'll be out of deep water soon. When the wind's in this direction and the tide's going out it usually gets a bit choppy.'

The bow dipped and icy cold salt spray swept over them. Water ran in rivulets down their oilskins and over the surfaces of the yacht as it rode the sea's switchback.

'You should see a red buoy to port,' she said.

He peered over the cabin top and caught another lash of spray in his face. 'I can't see a thing.'

'I may have come too far south. Never mind.'

'This is crazy. Why do we have to go by sea?'

'Quicker.'

'It's miserable and dangerous.'

'You're not enjoying it?'

'You're right. I'm not.'

The yacht bucked and tipped as she swung the tiller. A wash of frothing water sluiced over the gunwales.

'Your father is going to know this boat has been used,' he said.

'That won't matter. We'll have the money.'

'We're giving it back though. All except my thousand.'

'Are we?'

'Yes, we are.' He peered at her, trying to read the expression on her face. There was nothing soft or feminine about her as she stared ahead, searching for the buoy. Her eyes were narrowed and her lips thin; her face might have

136

been carved out of stone by someone wanting to give human countenance to his own private vision of cruelty.

'Have a look at the echo-sounder,' she ordered. 'Tell me what it's reading.'

He went below. The cabin seemed wonderfully warm and snug but as he steadied himself to read the instrument the yacht lurched and he felt the first stirrings of the nausea preceding seasickness. He knew that if he stayed too long in the confined, shifting little room he would be ill. It was better to suffer exposure to wind and rain. Clambering back he called, 'Just under three fathoms.'

'Good. I've spotted the buoy. The water is getting quieter.'

Mersea Island, flat and tree-covered, was visible ahead of them. The rain had slackened and the wind had dropped. Stephen felt better. Confidence, which had been trickling out of him like sand from a split sandbag, began to be restored. He had made up his mind. Once they were on dry land again he would say good-bye to Caroline. He was finished with her.

She could threaten him with false accusations of rape or genuine accusations of abduction but he wouldn't budge. Nothing she could say would shift him.

'Check the echo-sounder again, Stephen.'

'Right.'

He went below. I'll wipe the slate clean and start afresh, he thought. And then he paused. Wipe the slate was an uncomfortable reminder of Brown who liked to speak of wiping the cortical slate clean. Brown's cortical slate had been cleaned by death. The memory of a long sack-like shape disappearing into fenland bog came vividly to mind. It was a memory Stephen knew would haunt him. My cortical slate could use a wash, he thought. And he decided he would go back to the cottage and arrange for Brown's body to be exhumed and decently buried even if this would mean awkward police questions and the threat of court proceedings. If he was going to start a new life he didn't want to carry into it the burden of an uneasy conscience.

'What are you doing down there?'

He looked at the echo-sounder and could hardly believe his eyes. According to the instrument they were in less than four feet of water.

'Stop,' he shouted. 'Stop the engine!' He scrambled up to rejoin her. 'We must be almost aground. 'It's less than a fathom.'

'Thought so.' She cut the engine.

They were lying between mud banks and he could see the reed-covered entrance to a creek in the distance ahead. The rain, which a couple of minutes earlier had seemed to be fading into drizzle, was coming down in perpendicular shafts which silvered the sea.

'If you're wondering where the hard is, it's some way from here,' she said.

'The hard?'

'Never mind. I think we've got something caught on the bows. Can you take a look?'

Gripping the handrail he stood up and leaned over the side. It was difficult to see the bows and so he leaned at full stretch. He heard a thump and pain shot up his fingers, wrist and arm. Involuntarily he let go of the handrail. It needed only a slight push for her to tip him overboard.

The water seemed to hit him with a cold fist. He went under for a moment, and when he emerged he was coughing and spitting out salt water. He could feel something plastic under his feet. It was soft and oozed up to his ankles. Very slowly he turned to face the yacht and found he was looking up at his own shot-gun.

'Don't try to get on board,' she said.

'What the hell are you playing at?'

'How does it feel to be lost and helpless?'

'Let me back.'

'Not on your life. You're getting a taste of your own medicine.'

'Have you gone crazy?'

She gave a rather spiteful laugh. 'Whenever you can't understand something you call it crazy. No. Crazy I am not. You stranded me in a lot of filthy mud. I'm doing the same for you.'

He was aware of icy water cutting into his body and his right hand began to ache. But the discomfort was secondary to a sense of indignation and outrage. 'You planned this.'

'You bet I did. Back in that stinking room, locked in and helpless, I planned it. I only needed to get rid of Brown and he got rid of himself. Nobody makes me suffer without paying the price. Not you, not Brown, not my father. Nobody.'

The gun barrels pointed unwaveringly at his head. He wiped water which had trickled down his forehead out of his eyes and for a moment could hardly see for the sting of the salt.

'What's the matter,' she asked. 'Lost your tongue? Lost your persuasive powers?'

'Look, Caroline, I'm sorry I took you into that marsh. But it was before we . . . I mean, I thought we . . .'

'Thought! Thinking again. Well, you've got something to think about now. At least you've got a life-jacket. That's more than you gave me when you stranded me, blindfolded and at night.'

'For God's sake.'

'Not for God's sake, or anyone else's sake. The tide will soon be on the turn. You'd better make for land while you can – if you can. There are shallows and depths.'

Wavering only slightly in her aim she moved back and started the engine.

Panic obliterated his physical distress.

'Don't leave me!'

'I'm leaving, but before I go I'll fill in the picture so that you can have something to think about. You like thinking. Well, you can think about your own stupidity. When I used the phone I didn't say that my father had to go to a hotel in Colchester to wait for instructions. I gave a completely different place, hundreds of miles away. So don't waste your time rushing to the police with stories about a pill-box on the island. In fact, don't go to the police at all because I warn you – if you try to make any sort of noise I'll crucify you for raping me. So just crawl into a quiet corner and stay there. Okay?'

He began to struggle towards the yacht, his feet sinking into the mud with each step.

'What's the matter, Stephen? Don't you like your own medicine? You left me to flounder in the mud, now it's happening to you. At least you've got some idea where you are. I had none.'

'Please, Caroline. I'm begging you.'

'All right. Go on your knees and beg.'

The water was just below his chin. 'How can I,' he asked desperately.

She laughed. 'You do look funny. Go on. Beg. Submerge yourself.'

'You bitch!'

'Nasty. There's only one person who can call me names

140

and that's not you. He's more of a real man than you could ever be.' Holding the gun with its stock tucked under one armpit she reached down with the opposite arm for the gear lever. 'I'll tell you something else,' she said. 'You didn't even begin to succeed with me. Irving never left me. He was with me all the time. In spirit. And soon he'll be with me physically. I called him from the cottage when you were posting that letter and I called him again this morning.'

Stephen turned his head. The shore was a long way off and he was not a strong swimmer. The longer he stayed at the mercy of her taunts the less chance he would have of making land.

'Are you listening, Stephen? I'm going back to Irving. Why don't you follow? Grab me? Deprogramme me?'

He turned his back. It wouldn't be easy to reach land hampered by his gear but he was determined to survive. He made the first sluggish steps in shifting mud.

'Listen to me! I've not finished with you yet.'

He took no notice. Spray flailed close to him as he heard the whip-crack of gun-shots. He turned. She had used both barrels, but if he attempted to climb aboard she could easily club him.

'That's better,' she said. 'You don't walk away while I'm talking to you. I said I'm going back to Irving. You can report that to my father, if you've got the nerve. Tell him he'd better hire a better class of thug next time. You and Brown weren't up to the job of dealing with one defenceless woman.'

'I wish you luck, Caroline. God be with you.'

'God be with me. You stinking hypocrite. You'd kill me if you could.'

He shook his head.

'Here,' she said, 'this is no use to me. Take your symbol of manhood. You need all the manhood you can get.'

She hurled the gun at him. It fell short and sank.

He ducked below the surface and plunged forward with his good hand. He found contact and clung on to the gun.

As his head came up he could hear the sound of a receding engine. Without looking back, he began the struggle towards land.

CHAPTER THIRTEEN

'I don't get it,' said Samson, pacing his room.

'Unless you tell me I shan't get it either,' replied Shandy who was sitting in his swivel chair gently swinging from side to side as though she were already rocking a cradle.

'He's changed his tune completely. He wants us to call off the search. The case is closed.'

'Did he say why?'

'The ransom is being paid, or has been paid. He contradicted himself and wouldn't say whether it had been paid or was about to be paid. But on no account was I to take any further action.' He paused in his stride. 'And that is why I don't get it.'

'I don't either.'

'A hundred thousand pounds is a lot of money to be paid by a father who doesn't care all that much for his daughter. I could have sworn that no money would have passed. It doesn't add up to the man I pictured as her father and it doesn't add up to Camber.' He continued to pace up and down like some pachyderm restlessly awaiting an annual migration signal. 'Let us itemise the known facts. We are instructed by a man purporting to be the grandfather of Caroline Moore, aged nineteen, who has been . . .'

'Purporting?' queried Shandy.

'It passed my mind, as it must have passed yours, that

Camber was too one-dimensional to be true. And ex-army is a well-tried con-man front. It's the easiest impersonation in the world. I saw three alternatives. Either he was what he said he was, or he was one of the beneficiaries of Eventide Joy who somehow got wind of Caroline's disappearance and wanted to find her, or he was this fellow Irving O himself.'

He glanced at her as if to enquire whether she wished to add a fourth alternative. When she said nothing he continued. 'I never mentioned this to you, but I did a bit of research on Mr O while you were pursuing Stephen Hungerford. I got on to an old newspaper photo of him and it was nothing like the colonel. And so that alternative was ruled out. I still wasn't convinced that he might not have been a client of Eventide Joy who had been hooked by Caroline and found it easier to play the part of her grandfather rather than come out in the open and admit he was a dirty old man. This was one of the reasons why I asked him to tell me everything he knew about Caroline. He told me enough to make him undoubtedly her grandfather.' He gave a brief, sharp smile. 'That's what I mean by purporting. Now may I go on with itemising the facts?'

'Proceed,' she said solemnly.

'Caroline was abducted by men who have been hired by her parents to deprogramme her. We are instructed by someone who was instrumental in the abduction to find her. We are given the registration number of a van. Nothing more. Thanks to you we trace captors and captive to a remote cottage in East Anglia. But matters have become complicated by the fact that the abduction, although illegal in itself since Caroline was of age, but possibly excusable because it was arranged by her parents, has become a kidnap. There is a well-written ransom letter and there have been a couple of phone calls. Although we only have details of the calls at second-hand it sounds as though she spoke clearly and without hesitation. Her handwriting was un-flurried. She seems a cool customer.'

'Cool customer sounds like speculation, not fact,'

'It could be fact. Remember how tidy that cottage was. No clues left by a girl held down against her will except for the accidental clue of her hair in the bath plug-hole. Now, I don't believe her captors stood her in the bath and then cut her hair. Why should they? On the other hand, if she had decided to cut her own hair, and do it while she was in some privacy, she would either cut it in the bathroom or the lavatory.' He paused and looked at her with eyes which pierced from under heavy hoods. 'Right?'

She nodded.

'We know two men abducted her but the inference is that only one is now holding her. Mr X. Where is the other man?'

Shandy stopped swinging in the chair. 'Disposed of?'

Samson looked slightly vexed. 'You know I dislike euphemisms. Do you mean "killed"?'

'Sorry. Yes. Killed.'

'It could be that the two men simply quarrelled and one of them left saying he wouldn't have anything to do with the kidnap plan, but that would leave Mr X vulnerable to blackmail from his former colleague and a witness would be at large to testify against Mr X in any criminal proceed-ings. But there remains the mystery of the Wagner record sleeve. That was *disposed of*. Why? And why in a place no one would think of searching?'

'I think I'm beginning to get your drift. An ideal place to dispose of a body too.'

Samson began pacing again but he moved much more

slowly with arms clasped behind back. 'So,' he said, 'we now have one man and one girl. Is he still imprisoning the girl? What is the relationship between them?'

'What exactly did Camber say when you rang him?'

'Weren't you listening in?'

'No. I had a call on the other line. Paul. Just to check whether I'd be home in time for our anniversary next week.'

Samson sighed. 'You'd better go home. It's been a long day. And I don't want to be responsible for keeping a wife from her husband.'

She laughed and shook her head, and then brushed back hair which had fallen forward. 'You won't be. It does him good if I don't come running every time he calls.'

'Married life baffles me. It seems more like some elaborate game than two people in harness.'

'It's a beautifully elaborate game calling for lots of skill and bluff and very strict observance of a few ground rules. But we won't go into that. I'd like to know why Camber is opting out. Did he just say, "The ransom is being paid. Good-bye"?'

'More or less. I said I'd like to know where Moore kept his boat. He prevaricated a bit and then came out with it. The ransom had been or was about to be paid and would I please discontinue work on the case and send in my account.'

'What happened between him leaving us and you calling him?'

Samson stopped pacing. 'I don't like loose ends,' he said, 'and I don't like feeling hungry. If you won't go out for a Chinese takeaway I'll get it myself. I can't concentrate when I'm hungry.'

She stood up. 'You poor old thing. All right. I'll get something for us both.'

146

'You go home, Shandy. It's getting late.'
'It is late. See you in a few minutes.'

The delicate and appetising aroma of cooked Chinese food
made Samson's taste buds blossom so fast, and stimulated
his salivary glands to such frenzy, that he had to swallow
before speaking. 'That didn't take long.'

'I got the fixed meal for four people.'

'Well done. One for you and three for me?'

'Half each,' she said. 'Don't forget I have to eat for two
now.'

His face fell. 'You're teasing, I hope.'

'Of course. I like teasing that copious stomach of yours.
If you can manage enough for three people, good luck.'

She cleared her desk and laid out foil trays filled with
steaming food, and after handing him a spoon and a plate,
said, 'Tuck into that.' For herself she produced a pair of
chopsticks.

The spoon plunged into a tray containing shredded
pimento, bamboo shoots and Szechuen cabbage. 'You've
done well, Shandy.'

'I try to please.'

For a while they didn't speak but when she judged that
the razor-edge of his appetite had been blunted she said,
'You know we were wondering if the reason for wrapping
the ransom in something waterproof was because she might
be somewhere near water, a river or the sea?'

He absorbed the juices of roast duckling and lifted his
head. 'Yes?'

'And that's why it passed our minds that she might be
playing at hiding in the cupboard by hiding in her father's
boat.'

'What are you driving at?'

'It's just a thought. It came to me while I was waiting in the Golden Bamboo. There's a picture on the wall of a peasant wearing a sort of yoke across his shoulders with a bucket dangling at each end. It made me think of the well in front of the cottage. And then I thought how the well would be quite a good place to leave a ransom. In a bucket.'

Samson was masticating very slowly and his attention was riveted on her.

'It's an isolated place,' she went on. 'The kidnapper could watch through field-glasses and make sure that only one person came to the well and left. There's no chance of springing an ambush. It would be impossible for the police or anyone else to reach the cottage without being seen. The kidnappers could pick up the ransom whenever they wished.'

'Kidnapper. There is only one. If that.' Samson wiped his mouth with a paper tissue. 'Shandy, I think you have a not implausible theory.'

'Praise indeed!'

'When we've finished this I'll pay the colonel a visit.'

'With me.'

'Not with you. You are going home.'

'He might not see you. He'll say the case is closed.'

'It isn't closed for me. I don't like loose ends.'

'Nor do I.'

He gouged the dish of sweet and sour chicken so that not a morsel remained in the glittering tin-foil tray. 'I'm sorry, Shandy,' he said gently, 'but if I'm to get at the truth it's more likely he'll tell me, on my own, than if both of us were there . . . You still feel concerned on Caroline's behalf, don't you?'

She thought for a moment. 'Not really. Logic and reason tell me she is probably a pretty hot little manipulator herself. It's just that emotionally I feel some sympathy. I think she may have had a raw deal somewhere along the line.'

'Most of us can say that,' observed Samson.

'The colonel won't thank you for calling. He might even delay paying your fees.'

'I know. But I'm curious. It's my sense of curiosity which keeps me young and vital.'

She began to smile but suppressed it. 'Okay,' she said, 'I'll look out his address for you. And then I'll be on my way.'

'Finish your meal first.'

'No, thanks. I've had enough.' She stood up. 'Leave the dishes. I'll clear up in the morning.'

Colonel Camber lived on the fourth floor of a modern block of flats. Samson rang the bell and stood back knowing that before opening the door Camber would want to peer through the spy-hole. He stood well back so that the fish-eye magnification could accommodate his bulk.

The door opened. 'What are you doing here, Samson?'

'May I come in?'

'Suppose so.'

When he was seated in a room that was an overcrowded micro-world of trinkets, souvenirs and trophies of a lifetime of travel on army service, Samson stretched his short legs and said, 'Forgive me if this is presumption on my part but I think you still need my help.'

'What makes you think that?'

Samson drew a deep breath. 'You won't like me saying this, but I must be blunt. As a man who likes straight talk himself perhaps you won't hold it against me.'

The colonel, who was sitting erect on a hard straight-backed antique sewing chair, grunted and muttered, 'That sounds like waffle. Come to the point.'

'The point is that you were used – there's no other word for it – you were used by Caroline's parents to have her abducted. I believe, although you will probably deny it, that others have used you, with or without your knowledge.'

Camber's eyes began to bulge and his neck redden but he said nothing.

'For example,' Samson continued, 'I think Caroline used you when she was a child. She would come to you, apparently for comfort and affection, but also to score off her parents, particularly her father. Whether she succeeded, I don't know, but I guess she would dearly have liked to make her father jealous of her affection for you.'

'Absolute rubbish and tommy-rot!'

Samson gave a small pearly smile. 'I had an idea you might think it tommy-rot. But I also have an idea you are being used again. I don't know how, and I shan't know unless you tell me, but if I am right, and you are being used again, I think I might be able to help. Two heads are better than one, and I do have experience in dealing with extortion.'

The colonel's anger subsided; the flush faded from his neck and he stood up rather wearily. 'You're quite a sharp fellow, Samson. Not entirely on the ball, but quite sharp. . . . Hate this whole business. Want to get it finished and done with.' He moved towards a drinks cabinet the top of which was covered with pieces of native pottery, framed photographs and figures carved out of afrormosia. A large regimental photograph in a silver frame held pride of place in the dead centre. 'Like a drink? Gin? Whisky?'

'Whisky. On its own. Thank you very much.'

Camber poured a couple of measures. 'Yes,' he said. 'I dare say I have been used, as you put it. Never been very good at questioning other people's motives. Prefer orders and action to analysing motives. This do you?' He handed over a glass.

'Very well,' replied Samson, looking at a stiff measure of malt whisky with fond appreciation.

'Good health.' The colonel returned to his chair and sat down heavily. 'All right. You can help. But I'd better clear up a few things first.'

'Yes?'

The colonel spoke without raising his eyes from the glass which he held between cupped hands. 'May have given the impression that Mabel and Frank are reasonably happy together, or at least not unhappy. Not so. On the verge of separation.'

'On account of Caroline?'

'Not only her. They've been drifting apart. Chalk and cheese. Oil and water. They just don't mix. Plain fact is, Samson, I misled you slightly. It wasn't Frank who hired these fellows to brainwash Caro; it was Mabel. And she did it without his knowledge. Friends of hers had the same problem with their daughter and recommended these so-called technicians. It was on her behalf, not hers and Frank's, that I went to Tewkesbury to try and reason with her.'

'Did you know at that stage that your daughter had hired these men?' enquired Samson.

'I did not. It was only after they'd grabbed her that I found out what had happened. So did Frank. He was furious. He did agree to go up to the hideaway to check that things were all right. He didn't let on to the fellows that he and Mabel had quarrelled bitterly. Say that for him.

He kept up a united front for outsiders. But after he got back he washed his hands of the whole affair. Said she might be only nineteen but she was very adult in many ways and well able to look after herself. Told Mabel she had no right to interfere in Caro's life. Said that he wasn't interested in having her back, normal or otherwise. Caro had been home once since joining this Irving man. She and Frank had a row and she ran off. He told Mabel then that he never wanted to see or hear of her again.'

'He doesn't care about her at all?'

Camber shook his head sadly. 'Afraid so. Tragedy is, and God knows I'm no psychologist, I think deep down she cares about him.' He stood up and went to refill his glass. 'Families should be happy. What's the point of families if they're not happy? . . . Like another?'

'Thanks.' Samson surrendered his glass. 'What about the ransom demands? And who is paying, or has already paid?'

'Mabel is in a terrible state.' Camber handed over another generously filled glass. 'Frank no support at all. Won't pay a penny. She's scratched together four thousand and I've added ten. Can't manage more. Hope fourteen thousand will be enough.' He took out a handkerchief and blew his nose. 'Frank has all the money,' he went on. 'Working-class made good. Mabel and I typically middle-class. Just don't have the money. Standards, yes; money, no. But we mustn't get on that hobby-horse.'

'But no money has passed yet,' Samson queried.

'Not yet. It's here.' Camber waved his arm in the direction of a walnut cupboard which had its top surface covered by a gypsy caravan made from matchsticks, a piece of Japanese netsuke, a porcelain boat from Malta, a pair of silver spurs and a Malaysian wood carving of the Hindu goddess Kali wearing tiny skulls in a necklace.

'You intend handing it over,' asked Samson.

'Yes, I do.'

'When? Where?'

'When I got back from your office the phone was ringing. It was Mabel. She'd had the final demand. Unless the money was left in a certain place by a certain time Caro would be killed.'

'Who made the demand? Caroline?'

'Yes. She was being made to speak. Obviously someone with her. Forcing her.'

'And what did your daughter say?'

'She said it was hard to get a hundred thousand together but at least fourteen thousand would be handed over for a start.'

'What was the reply?'

'The reply was that it would do for a start.'

'Does Caroline know that her mother is doing all this and that her father won't have anything to do with it?'

'Good lord, no. The poor girl's suffering enough without being told of her father's attitude.'

Samson brooded for a moment and then asked, 'When Caroline said it would do for a start did she answer promptly or did she get instructions from someone?'

Camber frowned. 'Don't know. She must have asked whoever was with her.'

'And where is the money to be delivered?'

Camber's frown deepened. 'Very odd. Put in a bucket in a well, if you please.'

'And that's what you're going to do?'

'Certainly. Instructions very precise. Must be absolutely on my own . . .'

153

'You,' interrupted Samson. 'Won't she or Mr X be expecting her father?'

'No. Mabel said Frank was out of the country. Critical and urgent business. This is why only fourteen thousand available. Said I would be the courier.'

'I see. Where's the rendezvous?'

'Have to drive to this cottage where they once held Caro. Very exposed place. Be under observation all the time. After putting money in the bucket I have to leave. Any false move and Caro will die.'

A silence fell between them.

'Any ideas,' asked the colonel at length.

'I'm working on it. I think I'd better come along with you.'

Camber blinked as if a distracting light had suddenly been flashed in his face. 'My dear Samson, that's impossible. You'd be seen.'

Samson smiled. 'I shall be invisible. Can I have a look at your car? And then I'd like to borrow your phone to contact a chap who's rather clever at devising mechanical tricks.'

CHAPTER FOURTEEN

It took some time for Samson's friend, a man called Twyman, to connect the windscreen washer bottle under the bonnet to the carburettor, but having done this he filled the bottle with a mixture of oil and paraffin. The idea was that when Camber pressed the button on the dashboard, which should spray water on to the windscreen, a jet of oily mixture would be squirted into the carburettor. If the engine were running a pall of dark smoke would come out of the exhaust.

When the job was finished the colonel ran Samson back to his flat. It was two in the morning.

He had just set his alarm clock and climbed into bed when the phone rang. 'Samson,' he said.

'You sound fed up. Didn't it go well?'

'What the devil are you doing calling at this hour?'

'I've been calling every fifteen minutes. What happened?'

'You are a wife and an expectant mother,' said Samson in the sort of voice which defied denial. 'If you carry on like this you'll find yourself divorced before you have your baby.'

'Nonsense. I have a lovely and understanding husband.'

'Don't count on that,' said a man's voice in the background. This was followed by the sound of a kiss and then

Shandy's voice came through again and there was a faint chuckle in it. 'Now tell me what happened.'

'You were inspired in the Golden Bamboo. The ransom is to be put in a bucket in a well.'

'At the cottage?' Her voice was delighted.

'Yes, but Camber can only get fourteen thousand together. The father isn't interested. It's been Camber's and the mother's show throughout.'

'Poor Caroline.'

'He called her "poor Caroline". I'm not so sure she is poor Caroline.'

'You're letting him go ahead with it?'

'Not quite.'

A pause.

'Don't be rotten, Samson. Tell.'

'I feel like being rotten. I want to get some sleep.'

Nevertheless he told her of the instructions Camber had received and concluded, 'If he parks the car between the well and the front porch there's a chance that I'll be able to get out of the back unnoticed and make it into the cover of the porch.'

'You!' Her voice was unflatteringly incredulous.

'I'm as nimble as the next man.'

'It's taking a chance, isn't it?'

'Not if Camber pulls up closer to the porch than the well. Unless someone is inside the cottage it wouldn't be easy, even with binoculars, to see the rear door opening on the far side, the concealed side, particularly if we fix it that the rear windows are smeared or steamed up. And my friend Twyman has ingeniously adapted the windscreen-washer to provide a natural smokescreen.

'But what if there is someone inside the cottage?'

156

'Then there'll be a pretty brisk showdown, but I'm sure there won't be. The watch will be at a distance.'

'And so you wait until someone comes to collect the ransom and then you spring?'

'Like the tiger I am,' said Samson.

'It sounds great. When are you going?'

'I'm meeting Camber outside the block where he lives at seven. He'll have the car ready and waiting. I'll travel in front until we're nearly there and then I'll transfer to the back and keep, as they say, a low profile.'

'I don't know how I shall get through the day, waiting and wondering.'

'I'll ring when there's news.'

'Take care. I don't want to be without a boss.'

'You can spend the day lining up your successor.'

No sooner had he said this than Samson regretted it. The silence which followed had the curiously magnified effect which occurs when the other speaker has suddenly withdrawn behind some psychological barrier. When she spoke, Shandy's voice had a strained normality. 'I'll let you get to sleep,' she said. 'Good night.'

He had set the alarm to rouse him at five. It was a clock without a face, hands or digits, and it looked like any prettily carved wooden box which might be bought as a souvenir in any shopping arcade in any big city. But at exactly five o'clock the lid would spring open and a little bird which looked like a cross between a goldfinch and a robin would rise, open its beak and emit a piercingly trilling song. Samson, when demonstrating it to friends, called it his personal dawn chorus and he named the bird Billy after a canary he had kept as a pet when he was a child.

After Shandy's call he switched off the light and fell

asleep. A minute later, or so it seemed, the bird was singing. Samson switched on the light and said, 'Oh shut up, Billy-boy.' But he didn't check its song. He watched with affectionate, sleep-bleared eyes until, its duty done, the bird retired into its wooden nest and the lid clicked shut.

He rolled out of bed, yawned and stretched, and went into a complicated series of exercises. This was a new routine brought about by a periodic desire to regain some sort of physical fitness and it would continue until lazy self-indulgence had its inevitable triumph. After washing, shaving and dressing he went to the kitchenette. It was essential to start an arduous day with a satisfied stomach.

Two frying pans were necessary to accommodate the rashers of bacon and the eggs he required. Nearly half a loaf of bread was sliced for toast and the percolator filled with water to make at least three cups of coffee.

After despatching the food he asked himself if it wasn't a little foolish to face a long day on nothing more than a normal breakfast. Self-encouraged he took the remains of an apple pie from the refrigerator, doused it with cream and ate it. This done he used the rest of the bread loaf in making ham and cheese sandwiches which he wrapped in a polythene bag for use if he should feel peckish while hiding in the cottage.

Next he packed his voluminous overcoat with some of the tools of his trade including a .38 calibre automatic pistol. It had a long barrel for increased range as Samson reckoned that he would never need to use a pistol except at range. For anything less than thirty metres he relied on his hands and his wits.

The last item to be stuffed inside his overcoat was a bundle of newspaper cuttings. Having done this he phoned his own answer service and left a message.

'Hello, Shandy. This is the boss you don't want to be without. I didn't mean what I didn't say what you might have thought I meant. Be seeing you.'

Camber greeted him warmly. 'Spot on time, Samson. Well done.'

The car springs lurched as Samson climbed into the front passenger seat.

'Looks as though we're going to be lucky with the weather,' remarked Camber, engaging gear and letting off the hand-brake. 'Forecast for East Anglia is sunny and mild for time of year.'

The car moved slowly towards the forecourt exit. Camber jammed on the brakes as a figure suddenly stepped out from behind a pillar and barred the way.

'What the devil!'

'That's no devil,' said Samson. 'That's my secretary.'

'Good God! What's she doing here?' Camber wound down his window. 'Good morning, me dear. What's the trouble?'

'Could you open the back door, please.'

'Open? ... Right...'

He pulled back the catch and Shandy got into the car. 'We can go now,' she said.

Camber looked like a general who, in the middle of fighting a desert campaign, has just seen a fleet of submarines surface from the sand-dunes. 'What the devil's going on,' he asked.

'Didn't Mr Samson tell you? I've been working on this case from the beginning and he wanted me to come along.'

'This is no job for a woman. What were you thinking of, Samson? We can't take her.'

'We've been outmanoeuvred, Colonel.'

159

'It's impossible. It'll be difficult enough to get you into the cottage unseen. But two of you!'

'She *has* been working on the case,' said Samson, 'and in fact she guessed that the ransom might be put in a bucket before you told me about it.'

'It was no guess,' interrupted Shandy. 'It was a deduction.'

Camber looked nonplussed. 'I'm not at all sure this whole thing won't blow up in our faces. If these crooks see either one of you it could go badly for Caro.'

'Then we must make sure they don't see us,' said Samson. 'I've brought along some paste to smear the rear windows with.'

'I don't like taking a woman along.'

'And if you leave the engine running at the cottage while you go to the well it'll look as though you've been running on full choke or there's something wrong with the mixture control.'

'No place for a woman.'

'But a volunteer is worth ten pressed men, Colonel,' observed Samson.

'That's true. Very true. All right then. Against my better judgment she can stay.'

The car moved forward again.

Samson turned to look at Shandy. She winked at him. It was difficult to see whether he winked back but one of his hood-like eyelids may have sagged. .

Once they were out of London's traffic the journey was smooth and easy. Camber told some army anecdotes and evoked a picture of horseplay at mess parties, jokes played on rookies and bizarre native customs.

'Fascinating,' said Shandy after hearing how the colonel's batman had been obliged to marry the daughter of a tribal chief in the Gold Coast. 'But what exactly did you do in the fighting line?'

The silence which ensued was at first unremarkable and then it became awkward, embarrassing and, finally, painful. 'Tell the truth, me dear,' said Camber at last, 'I was the most damned unlucky fellow in the fighting services. Travelled a lot before the war, saw lots of foreign parts, and that was good. In North Africa at the outbreak of hostilities but as soon as things hotted up there I was posted to India. Thought I was going to get into the Burma campaign when that hotted up but I was posted to the Gold Coast. Protested. Said I wanted to see action. Fat lot of good my protest did. Got posted to the bloody Bahamas! Same story after the war. In Aden and Cyprus but got moved out just before the real trouble began. Ridiculous really. I only joined in the first place to see a bit of action.'

'What a shame,' she said sympathetically.

'You're right. But all the same they were great days. A man's life. No doubt of it.'

'If that's a man's life,' Shandy asked, 'what is a woman's life?'

'In the home,' he replied without hesitation. 'Child rearing. Home fires burning and all that.'

The following dialogue kept Samson amused all the way to Cambridgeshire. It ended with Shandy saying rather plaintively, 'I'm not really Women's Lib.'

A comment by Camber about how quickly the journey had passed gave Samson the opportunity to tell them about an experiment involving car travel in which it had been demonstrated that time appears to pass more slowly when one is going through strange territory.

Camber thought about this and said, 'Never been in

these parts before but time's gone fast. Damn silly experiment.'

In the back of the car Shandy laughed.

As they passed through Fen Soken she said, 'That's where I bought the aspirins,' and when they reached the yellow-brick houses she said, 'Colditz.'

'If you pull off the road along here,' said Samson, 'I'll attend to the windows.'

Camber slowed down and turned into a rutted farm track. 'Will this do?'

'Perfect.'

'If so much wasn't at stake,' said Camber, 'I'd be really enjoying myself. Action at last.'

As he drove along the causeway leading to the cottage Camber kept up a running commentary.

'Very flat. Excellent visibility. See for miles. Man on a tractor to far left. Estimate his distance at eight hundred yards at roughly ten o'clock.'

'Get into your gun turret, man,' whispered Shandy giving Samson a nudge. He was lying on the seat and she was crouching beside him.

'Just passed a sign saying "Private property, no access",' announced Camber. 'Approaching rough country. Marshy. Pools of water. Must have had a lot of rain here lately. Not a sign of life anywhere. Cottage dead ahead. This road very exposed. If anyone's watching they'll see us.'

'Isn't it about time you pressed the button,' asked Samson.

'Right. Pressing button now . . . Nothing happening.'

'Give it a chance, Colonel.'

'Worked all right when we tested it. Better slow down. Getting close anyway. Your description spot on, Samson.

162

Can see exactly where to go. Why isn't that damn exhaust smoking? No sign of life in the cottage. Sure you were right about that. It's the one place they wouldn't be holding Caro. Fifty yards to well. Where's that bloody smoke got to?'

'Perhaps there's a strong wind and it's blowing the smoke too low for you to see in your mirror,' suggested Shandy.

Samson eased himself into a position to open the door. With some difficulty, and clasping her stomach protectively, Shandy squeezed back to give him as much room as possible.

'Do we still go if there's no smoke cover,' she whispered.

'I'm going. You stay. That's an order.'

'No deal. It's both or no one.'

The car had slowed to a crawl.

'You'll do as I . . .' Samson began but he was interrupted by an excited bellow from the front.

'She's smoking! The old girl's smoking!'

'That settles it,' said Shandy.

'Ready to go,' asked Camber, putting on the brakes.

'Ready,' replied Samson.

'All the best. Contact me when you can. Good luck.'

Obscured by a blanket of black smoke Samson and Shandy scrambled out of the car. Colonel Camber reached for a parcel wrapped in a waterproof sheet, climbed out and walked, shoulders back and chin out, to the well. After placing the parcel in the bucket he lowered it until it was almost touching the water. Having done this, he marched back to the car, got in and drove away.

'Except for a dodgy moment with the smoke that went well,' said Shandy. 'Like clockwork.'

'Anything that goes like clockwork must go well,' replied Samson favouring her with a smile.

After a check that the cottage had been undisturbed since their previous visit they stationed themselves in a bedroom which had a view over the well and down the causeway.

Time passed. Every so often one of them would go to a back room to see whether there was any sign of activity at the rear of the cottage. Except for wheeling seagulls there was none.

'As a matter of interest what will you do if they come in an armoured car, grab the bucket and leave?'

'Good question,' replied Samson.

'Then it deserves a good answer.'

Samson assumed the magisterial air of a man about to give an important judgment. 'We'll play it by ear.'

'That's not a very good answer.'

'It's the best you'll get.'

'I reckon they'll come at night. By stealth. And we shan't see a thing. In the morning we'll find the bucket gone. Incidentally, I can't understand you letting him put all that money into it.'

'I didn't.' Behind envelopes of flesh Samson's eyes twinkled. 'I switched packets.'

'When?'

'Last night he showed me his packet and when I got back to my flat I made up one of the same size full of cut-up newspapers. Then, while you were drawing him into a Women's Lib versus Male Pig contest I manage to take the wrapping from his packet and put it on mine.'

'And I never noticed . . . Samson, look!'

She was staring out of the window. A small red van was racing along the causeway. Samson raised and then lowered

164

his field-glasses. 'It's a Post Office delivery van,' he said, 'unless our gang of two has changed the colour of their van and stuck the royal cypher on it.'

They watched, each concealed by a curtain, as a postman parked near the well, and hurried to the front door. The click of a letter flap was followed by the sound of his retreating footsteps.

Shandy went downstairs and brought back a letter.

'It's addressed to a Mr C. R. Fastnet and looks like a demand for rates.'

Samson grunted. 'Home from home,' he said.

'Oh well, it was a diversion.'

'It may seem like a long day, Shandy.'

Shortly after this she made two cups of coffee and he ate his sandwiches.

After a long silence he said, 'Which would you prefer? Boy or girl?'

'I haven't really thought about it. Girl, I think. Would you mind being godfather to a girl?'

'Godfather?'

'I know it's a bit premature, but would you?'

A look of pleasure swept across Samson's face. 'I've never been asked to be a godfather before. I'd be delighted.'

'Good. But I'm surprised you've never been asked before.'

'I'm not the family type.'

She glanced at him sideways. 'I'm not so sure. I've sometimes seen you looking quite paternal. You've never wanted a family of your own?'

He smiled and shook his head.

'Or marry?'

'Shandy, you're probing. It's a long story and not for today. Can't I tempt you to this last sandwich?'

*

Halfway through the afternoon she laughed and said, 'I've just had a wild fantasy. Do you want to hear it?'

'I have a choice?'

'Don't be mean. We're not really waiting for a ransom to be collected. We're a couple of actors waiting to go on stage for a song and dance act, and you're going to start with "There's a hole in the bucket, dear Shandy" and I ad lib with "Will the ransom fall through it, dear Samson". and so on . . . Come to think of it, it isn't as funny as I thought it would be.'

He gave a wan smile. 'I've never cared for that song.'

'That's because it pokes fun at a lazy man and you . . .' She stopped speaking and cocked her head to one side. 'What's that,' she asked.

A faint whirring sound grew louder. It was coming from behind the cottage. Shandy hurried into the other room.

'Fasten your safety belt,' she called in an excited voice. 'It's a helicopter, and it's making for here.'

Within a few seconds the noise was many decibels above comfort as the pilot increased engine pitch to hover above the well.

Samson stood well back and focused his field-glasses.

'I've got it's number,' said Shandy, standing beside him again. 'We'll be able to trace it.'

As they watched, the observer's side door opened and a rope ladder was uncoiled.

'They're going to lift the bucket,' said Samson.

'What do we do about that?'

'There seem to be five people on board,' he said. 'Four men and, if I'm not mistaken, a woman with short hair. It could be Caroline . . . And one of the men is like the picture I've seen of Irving.'

A man shinned down the ladder and began to cut the well rope. Above, standing in the door by a winch, another man held a sub-machine-gun. It was trained on the cottage.

'For God's sake don't let them see you,' said Shandy urgently.

'They won't. It's darker in here than out.'

The rope was severed and the man started to wind it round one arm. Samson put down the field-glasses and grabbed his .38 automatic. He slipped off the safety catch. The man with the sub-machine-gun had put it away and was winching up the ladder.

With his free hand Samson picked up a heavy vase. He had only to hurl it through the window and jump forward to fire through the hole in the broken glass and within two seconds, if he scored a hit on the engine, the helicopter blades would go into auto-rotation and the craft would drop to earth its blades flailing like a powerless windmill.

'No,' he said aloud. And he replaced the vase and put on the safety catch.

'Too risky?'

He nodded.

The man who had been lowered was on board again together with the bucket.

'If I'd hit the engine,' explained Samson, 'it would have dropped like a stone but probably landed the right way up. The people inside would stand a chance of getting away with injuries. But if I'd hit a blade anything might have happened. I wouldn't give them much chance of staying alive.'

The observer's door was closed and the helicopter began to rise. The pilot turned his craft towards the north-west over the tract of marshland. It had gone less than a mile when, without warning, it keeled over sideways. Simultaneously a sharp, cracking sound could be heard above the engine noise. A moment later it went into an erratic topsy-turvy spin like some giant dragonfly disorientated and dying from a massive spray of insecticide.

It hit the ground at speed, its engine was silenced, and a huge gout of marsh mud rose slowly into the air.

Samson ran down the stairs and out of the cottage.

CHAPTER FIFTEEN

When Stephen Hungerford reached land he lay exhausted in a grassy hollow. When he had recovered enough to stand up without his legs feeling like soft putty he took off his life-jacket and oilskins. He picked up his gun and wrapped it carefully in the discarded oilskins. Having done this he took a last look out to sea.

The first of the Brent geese had arrived at their winter quarters and he could see a few feeding on the mud. Beyond this the sea was bleak and bare to the horizon but in the sky above a few streaks of blue were appearing between shifts of grey cloud.

Tucking the gun under his arm he began walking inland.

Four hours later he was opening the door of his London pad, a flat in Balham. Anger which had built up on the journey was in full flood. If Caroline had walked in he would have smashed the gun over her head. She had kicked his pride, trampled on his self-esteem, and a need for revenge seemed to burn like acid in his stomach. It was only after a long, hot bath that his fury, like his tired limbs, was eased. He lay down on his bed intending to rest for a few minutes before going out for a meal and fell instantly into a deep sleep.

When he woke it was night and light from street lamps

cast a pale square on the wall beside him. His anger had been replaced by a sense of loss. With a little luck things could have been so much better. In some ways they were two of a kind – lost lady, lost man, she had said. He remembered their love-making and felt sad.

What next? It was time for a new direction. The money he was owed by Caroline's father was a write-off – he hadn't earned it anyway – and rather than brood over past mistakes it would be better to plan for future achievements. If he could obtain a grant for a research project he would start collecting data for a definitive social history of the fen people and he would form a pressure group to strive for improved conditions. Other underprivileged areas had powerful lobbies but where was the man who would stand up and shout for Hereward's people?

The tenancy of the cottage still had a week to run. In his haste to clean up the place and dispose of Brown's body he had forgotten that some of his books on fen history were in the lounge. He decided to collect these and, at the same time, to check that there were no traces of Brown. The idea, when he was on the yacht, that he might have the body exhumed had been foolish. Difficult questions would be asked; he might even be charged with attempting to conceal a death. Brown was dead. He would rest as much in peace beneath marsh mud as in a cold municipal cemetery.

Stephen drew the curtains and unwrapped his gun. It would need cleaning but there was no reason why it shouldn't shoot as well as ever. He might spend two or three days at the cottage and do some wildfowling.

Feeling more cheerful, he began to get ready to go out for a meal. Tomorrow would see the start of a new chapter in his life. He was whistling an Elvis tune as he left the flat.

He arrived at Fen Soken the following afternoon. It might have been possible to scrounge a lift to the cottage from one of the villagers but he decided to walk across fields and marsh. Walking was an enjoyable exercise and he liked the sense of physical fitness it gave. After provisioning himself at the village store he set off, carrier bag in one hand and gun under the other arm.

The violent anger against Caroline had dissipated in the resolve to take a new direction in life, and as he strode along a field path which would shortly peter out into unreclaimed fen he was wondering whether to approach Fastnet, the cottage owner, with a proposal to form a society to promote research into endemic fenland illnesses so as to discover whether there was evidence to link these with the transmission of recessive genes common among fen-folk.

He was following a way known only to himself and Fen Soken's oldest inhabitant, threading through dank pools of water, damp soil squelching underfoot, when he saw a helicopter. He watched in fascination as it flew over the cottage and then hung in the sky like a kite.

At first he thought that perhaps the pilot was lost and had stopped to get his bearings and then he saw a man descending a rope like a spider on a cobweb. This must be a planned visit, not some chance happening, but who would want to come to the cottage in a helicopter?

While they were on the yacht Caroline had mentioned that Irving owned a helicopter.

And then Stephen understood; everything fell into place. The ransom must have been paid and Caroline was going to hand it over to Irving. Probably he was in the helicopter with her.

He was stung into fury at the thought that she had used the cottage as a place to collect the ransom. It was part of a scheme designed to humiliate him even further. The landscape blurred and he had difficulty in unfastening the straps of his gun-bag. Then everything cleared to needle-sharp perspective. The helicopter was approaching. He raised his gun and, as if it were a game bird, he swung the gun through the arc of its flight trajectory and fired.

For a moment nothing happened and he thought he had missed. But suddenly the helicopter veered and turned upside down. He watched with a sort of joyful horror as it plunged to earth.

Jumping and side-stepping he was soon at the place where it had fallen. Already there was nothing to be seen but a pair of wheels poking out of the marsh like two jugglers' saucers on sticks. One wheel was spinning slowly.

He knew there was no hope for the occupants. If any survived they would be drowned in mud.

I must get out of here, he thought. Nobody will know I did it.

And then – he could scarcely believe his eyes – he saw a big, fat man who seemed to be dancing his way towards the scene. 'Stop,' he yelled before he could think.

The man stopped.

'You'll end up in bog. It'll suck you down. Stay where you are.'

'What about them?' shouted the man.

'They've had it,' answered Stephen, 'and so will you if you come any nearer.'

Samson had been halted on the edge of the mire which covered Brown's corpse.

The crash had been seen by a farmhand. Within a few minutes a police car was driving along the causeway.

A surprised sergeant found three people standing on the verge. There was a portly middle-aged man, a young fair-haired man holding a shot-gun, and a young woman who was obviously pregnant.

The older man spoke. 'You'd better radio for the fire brigade or whoever has equipment to raise a helicopter buried in swamp, Sergeant. We three will come with you to the police station. We have statements to make.'

Camber listened to Samson's account with tears in his eyes.

'I don't know what Mabel will say, but I can tell you this. It grieves me that Caro will never know that I didn't betray her willingly.'

'If it's any comfort,' said Samson, 'I'm sure death was instantaneous.'

'Loved Caro. Would have given my life for her. Why not? I'm old. Not much use now.'

Samson placed a hand on the other man's shoulder. 'That's defeatist talk, Colonel.'

Camber braced himself. 'You're right, dammit. Would never do for the other ranks to hear me talking like this.'

Samson removed his hand and took a package from his pocket. 'It's a small consolation but the ransom didn't go down with them.'

'Switched them, did you? I've said it before but I'll say it again. You're a smart fellow.' He tossed the package on to a table. 'Mabel will be glad to get hers back.'

'And you,' asked Samson.

'It'll be useful. Fat to live on. Haven't got all that much

173

capital and what I had I was going to leave to Caro. Have to make a fresh will. Still, that's my problem.' He extended his hand. 'Thanks for all you've done. I'll recommend you like a shot to anyone who needs a private detective.'

Stephen Hungerford pleaded not guilty to murder but guilty to the lesser offence of manslaughter. The plea was accepted. He was sentenced to six years' imprisonment.

In due time Shandy gave birth to a daughter. Samson visited the maternity ward and with an embarrassed gesture presented her with a bouquet of flowers.

'They're beautiful,' she said, placing them on a locker by her bed.

He sat down on a chair a few sizes too small for his girth and weight. It creaked.

'Even chairs protest these days,' he remarked.

She smiled. 'It's the Age of Protest. You should have heard Kimberley when she was born.'

'Is that what you're calling her?'

'Don't you like it?'

'Will she?'

'It's a good thing I know you well, otherwise I might be offended . . . How's the temp going?'

'She's not a patch on you.'

'That's better. That's what I like to hear.'

Samson looked round. At the next bed a man and woman were holding hands and talking in whispers. He pulled his chair closer to Shandy. 'Did you read that he got six years?'

'Yes. I felt a bit sorry for him. I think he loved her. She didn't love him.'

174

'You saw that her father has had a nervous breakdown and is in hospital?'

'I did.' She paused before saying, 'When a person goes against nature, he's in trouble . . . I never figured out Caroline. She's never been more than a silhouette, although I did feel sympathy for her at one time. But I suppose being a silhouette is the fate of people like her, self-centred people. They are shadows more than substance to everyone except themselves.' She smiled and looked fondly at the fat detective sitting beside her.

He patted his stomach. 'Substance,' he said.